I IS
SOMEONE
ELSE

By the same author:

O'Driscoll's Treasure
Wings to Fly

I IS SOMEONE ELSE

PATRICK COOPER

Andersen Press • London

For Jet

First published in 2003 by
Andersen Press Limited,
20 Vauxhall Bridge Road, London SW1V 2SA
www.andersenpress.co.uk

British Library Cataloguing in Publication Data available
ISBN 1 84270 306 4

*Photograph of Arthur Rimband on cover reproduced with the permission of the
Musée Arthur Rimband, Charleville-Mézières, France*

Typeset by FiSH Books, London WC1
Printed and bound in Great Britain by Mackays of Chatham Ltd.,
Chatham, Kent

'For "I" is someone else... That much is clear to me: I am a spectator at the blossoming of my own thought: I look at it and listen to it: I make a sweep with the baton and down in the depths the symphony begins to stir.'
Arthur Rimbaud

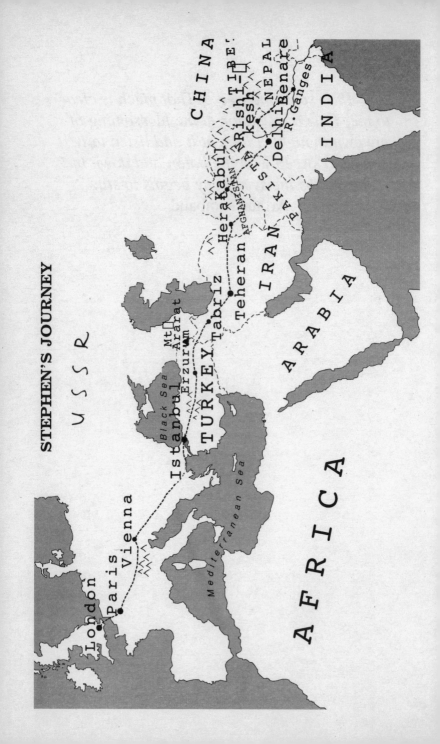

Part 1:
The Smell of Freedom

The real travellers are those who leave for the sake of leaving.
Charles Baudelaire

Chapter 1

Stephen sniffed the sea-spray. It smelled of freedom.

It was the 3rd April 1966, and he was going abroad on his own for the first time. A few hours before, his mother had set him on the train at Victoria with his suitcase and his sandwiches, and kissed him on the cheek – a rare kiss, that made him feel uncomfortable. Now he was on the ferry on his way to France, where he was to stay with a family to improve his French. In a few more hours Thierry, his French exchange, would meet him at Charleville Station and take him home with him. But for now he was his own master.

He felt nervous and elated.

There weren't many people on the deck – it was too cold. He did up the buttons on his anorak against the wind, and enjoyed the sun on his face. Then he noticed her.

She was hanging over the rail looking out to sea, and he watched her profile, and her hair blowing across it, and the way she flicked it back with long fingers.

She was the most beautiful girl he had ever seen. But she was too old for him. She'd never be interested, even.

She turned round, so that he could see her full face. She was looking for someone.

Her eyes met his. And instead of looking away immediately, she blinked and looked at him harder. And then, as if she couldn't help it, she smiled.

She turned back and watched the sea again.

Stephen's heart was palpitating. He needed to calm down. He went inside, and found the toilet.

The toilet was disgusting and smelled of sick, but there was a basin with hot water and a mirror.

Why had she smiled at him? He looked at himself in the mirror. He wasn't bad-looking, he knew that. He probably looked a bit older than his age, and he didn't have terrible acne or anything, just the odd spot. All the same, she couldn't fancy him, could she? But why else would she smile at him?

No, it wasn't possible, a girl like that. She was sophisticated and beautiful, and she could have any man she wanted. She'd never be interested in him, not in his wildest dreams.

He combed his hair and then ruffled it again, making a face in the mirror. Without thinking, he started to squeeze a spot on his chin, then wished he hadn't, because it left a red blotch that was worse than the spot. He splashed water on the blotch, and accidentally wetted his jumper.

Why *had* she smiled at him?

Would she smile again?

He dried himself as best he could on the pull-out towel and went back outside.

She was no longer alone. She was standing in the prow with the spray splashing behind her and gulls wheeling, posing for a man wearing white flared jeans and an embroidered sheepskin waistcoat, who was taking photos of her.

She looked more beautiful than ever.

Stephen sat down where he could see them out of the corner of his eye, and pretended to read his book.

The girl knew he was back. She glanced at him, and then she looked again.

The man finished taking photos and put away his camera. As he did so, the girl bent down and whispered to him, then looked towards Stephen. The man stood up, shouldering his camera case, and looked hard at him too. Then he walked over to him, the girl following.

'Hi!' he said. 'Sorry! We were really staring at you there!'

He grinned at Stephen. It was a disarming, boyish grin, and his eyes twinkled. Stephen smiled back, not quite knowing what to say.

'Anyway, my name's Jerry, and this is Astrid.'

'I'm Stephen,' said Stephen. He wondered whether to shake their hands, but it didn't seem the thing to do.

'Good to meet you,' Jerry continued. 'I know this sounds ridiculous, but you really remind us of a friend of ours. It's kind of uncanny – you've got just the same face. Astrid thought you were him for a moment, but you're not, obviously. You could be his kid brother though. It's that close a likeness. So I wondered if you'd mind if I took a couple of photos of you, so we can show him when we next see him…'

'Oh, yes, okay,' said Stephen, confused for a moment.

And then he stopped. What was the man talking

about? Someone who looked like him? Who might be his older brother?

What if it was Rob he meant?

Just at the thought his blood started racing. In the last few months he had started to forget about Rob, to get on with his own life without him. Of course, this was probably nothing to do with him, just one of those coincidences. But he had to ask. He had to know.

'Did you . . .' he asked. 'I mean, this friend of yours, he isn't called Rob is he?'

Jerry and Astrid looked at each other.

'That's right,' said Jerry. 'Rob. He's called Rob.'

'Has he got a chipped front tooth?'

Jerry nodded. His grin was growing ever wider.

'I think we've made a discovery here, Astrid. He's your brother, right?'

'Yes,' Stephen mumbled. 'My brother . . .'

Adrenaline was pumping all round his body, in a strange mixture of emotions. So Rob was alive, after all. Well, he'd never doubted it really. He turned away and looked out to sea, overwhelmed by the onrush of memories:

Rob and his mother, shouting at each other in the kitchen, just before he left for the last time; Stephen didn't know what it was about, and he didn't care – his mother and Rob had always argued. It was his father he was watching, standing ineffectually in the background with a look on his face that was sad, world-weary, long beyond anger . . .

... Then the policeman – that was much later – uncomfortable in an armchair in the drawing room, after his mother reported Rob missing:

'I'm sorry, there's nothing we can do. A lad his age . . . as you say, he could be anywhere. I'm sure he's come to no harm. We'll keep the details on our file, and let you know if we hear anything.'

A single tear rolled down his mother's cheek, and a greyness seemed to settle around her . . .

. . . And Rob, always the big brother, fighting, swearing, playing guitar, reading poetry with him. On the last night of his last visit – only Stephen didn't know it was to be the last – they had walked together into town. Not that there was anything to do there, it was just to get out of the house. Turning in the streetlamp, Rob looked at Stephen intensely: 'Hey, bro, there's a big world out there, you know!'

Stephen turned back to Jerry and Astrid. Were these glamorous people really Rob's friends? They seemed to think so.

Jerry clapped his thigh in delight.

'Too much! It must be the same guy.'

Astrid smiled her dazzling smile.

'I told you! He's so like. Only maybe even cuter.'

'Your brother – how old is he?'

Stephen didn't have to think. Rob was four years older than him. He always had been and he always would be.

'Nineteen.'

'It is! It *must* be same guy! Hey, you know, this is amazing. Why don't I take a couple of pictures, then we can go inside, score a coffee, and talk, right?'

'Rob – what a great guy!' said Jerry. 'He really is your brother, isn't he? I mean, we haven't got the wrong person, or anything?' He looked at Stephen closely. 'No, you're really just like him – that nose! The eyes too. Now I come to think of it, he told me about you. He said how much he missed you. You hear much from him?'

Stephen shook his head.

'No, we never hear. We knew he'd gone abroad – he sent postcards home occasionally. Then he stopped. We haven't heard anything for ages. My mother won't talk about him any more. She thinks he's dead.'

Jerry shook his head.

'That's terrible. I'd never have thought Rob would have done a thing like that. There must be a reason . . .'

'Where is he?' Stephen broke in. 'Where's he living? When did you last see him?'

Jerry was startled by the intensity of Stephen's questions. He looked at him sharply, then sipped his coffee.

'Rob? Rob's in Istanbul, I guess. I mean for sure. That's where he was going. That's where we're going now, actually. Hey, I just had an idea. Why don't you take a ride with us?'

'To Istanbul?'

'To Istanbul! It'd be cool. You'll get to see Rob, and you can tell him yourself what a shit he's been, not writing to you and that. You can check him out, get his address, come back after a few days on the Orient Express. Simple.'

Stephen tried to gather his thoughts. It was all too much for him to take in at one go. He had always thought deep down that Rob would turn up again one day, but to know that he was alive, to know for certain, that was something else. And who was this man, Jerry? Was he a 'hippy'? Hippies were supposed to have long hair, and Jerry's was very short, but there was something about him, and the way he spoke – all that American jargon.

Well, Rob was probably a hippy by now too. Drugs and Free Love, that was just his style. And this man, Jerry, might easily be a friend of his. There was no doubt about it. And so might Astrid.

He glanced at her. She had opened a German magazine, and was flicking through it at the same time as she listened to their conversation. Just the sight of her gave his heart a little flutter. If he went, he'd be in a car with her, all the way to Istanbul.

He pulled himself together. He had to be sensible.

'I've . . . I've got to go to France,' he said.

Jerry didn't seem to have heard him. He tugged at Astrid's arm.

'Hey, Astrid, what do you say? Why don't we take Stephen along with us to Istanbul, get him back together with Rob?'

Astrid looked straight at Stephen with big, green eyes. Her lips parted, showing little white teeth, though she didn't quite smile.

'I think that's a great idea, Jerry darling,' she said slowly.

Stephen pulled his eyes away, and looked down at his coffee.

'I can't,' he said again. 'I have to go to France.'

'France? What are you going to France for?'

'To learn French. They're expecting me.'

'Fair enough,' said Jerry. 'Can't argue with that. But it's your brother we're talking about here. And you haven't seen him for...'

'Nineteen months,' said Stephen.

'Right,' said Jerry. 'That's a long time.'

'I have to go to the French family,' said Stephen. 'My mother'd have a heart attack if I didn't turn up.'

And that was only the beginning of it. And yet. And yet, wouldn't she – especially she – want to know that Rob was still alive?

'Your mother? Yes, I can understand that. Too bad!'

Jerry shook his head, accepting Stephen's refusal.

'It's a pity, but there we go. Why don't you write a letter to send with us to Rob? He'll write back, I'm sure he will.'

Stephen wished he was as sure as Jerry. Why hadn't Rob written all this time, if he was alive and well? He knew where to write to.

'Do you know his address?' he asked.

Jerry laughed, as if Stephen had said something ridiculous.

'Address? No, I don't know his address. But we'll find him. Probably run into him straight away outside the Blue Mosque. If not we'll put a note in the Pudding

10

Shop. Everyone checks in there sooner or later. Hey, pity you can't come. You'd have a good time, you know that? There's quite a world out there.'

Stephen bought a postcard of the boat from the purser's office, to send to Rob.

What could he say?

He tried:

Dear Rob, just met these friends of yours on the ferry, who say they're going to see you soon. Please write and tell us you're still alive. We all really miss you.

It sounded lame.

They'd left the cafeteria, and they were sitting in the lounge. Jerry and Astrid were lying back on the seat opposite Stephen. Jerry was lost in thought, his eyes drifting idly round the room, while Astrid snuggled into his arm with her eyes closed. Her hair fell about her shoulders, and a sunbeam caught her face, making it glow gold.

Through the window, the French coast was approaching rapidly.

Stephen tore his postcard into small pieces and put them in the ashtray.

They'd be gone soon, these people, and that would be that. He'd never see them again, and he'd probably never see Rob again either. He'd go to Thierry's and then back to school at Grindlesham, back to the Wart...

He shuddered momentarily at the thought. But he'd have to go back there. There was no way out. No way. Unless...

He looked at Jerry and Astrid.

Did these people really know Rob?

Did they really know his big brother? His big, brilliant brother, who won all the school prizes and captained the Colts' cricket team? His brother Rob, who everyone knew was destined for big things, and then threw it all away?

Perhaps they'd confused him with somebody else. Even if Stephen did go with them, he'd get there and find somebody he'd never seen before in his life.

He couldn't be sure though. He just couldn't be sure.

That was the worst of it, not knowing. That had been the terrible thing from the beginning, when the postcards stopped. He hadn't minded up till then. But not knowing where Rob was, whether he was alive or dead, that had been the hardest thing to bear.

'He's dead for me,' his mother said, with her grim set of the lips. And after that she refused to talk about him, though Stephen was sure she thought about him all the time. Her darling boy. Her favourite.

'As long as I'm coming top and winning prizes, that's all she cares about!' Rob had said to him that last holidays. 'She doesn't love me. She loves my success. You'll see.'

But it wasn't true. Stephen knew it wasn't true. Because everyone loved Rob, and they couldn't help it. Stephen had always trundled behind him in his shadow. And when Rob went, his shadow only grew longer and darker.

This chance would not come again.

He felt calm and clear. He knew what he had to do.

There was an inaudible announcement on the loud speakers. Jerry stirred and looked out of the window.

'Hey, man, we're getting there. You got a note for us to take to Rob, or something?'

'I've changed my mind,' said Stephen. 'I'd like to come.'

Chapter 2

Dear Mum and Dad,
I'm not going to Thierry's family now, because something has
happened, and I am going to Istanbul instead to try to find
Rob. I met a couple on the ferry who are good friends of his,
and they say he is in Istanbul and they are going there and
will give me a lift. They have a car. So with a bit of luck I
will see Rob, and then we will all know for sure where he is
and that he is all right.

I know you will be cross, but I have to do this. Otherwise
we'd never know. I will come straight back on the train, I
promise, and if I am back in time I can go to Thierry then. I
will be quite a seasoned traveller by then!

I have enough money, and if I don't the man who is giving
me a lift will lend me some. Please don't worry about me, as
I am all right, and know what I am doing.

Love from
Stephen

The Green Bus was waiting.

It wasn't really a bus, but a VW combi van, hand-painted with fronds of vegetation, as if it was covered with vines. It was hip, and it was smart as well. Rather like Jerry and Astrid, Stephen thought.

They drove off the ferry, through the customs, who eyed them suspiciously before waving them on as if the whole business was too much trouble, then cruised past the long row of hitchhikers, holding signs saying 'Frankfurt' or 'Paris' or 'Vienna' or 'Katmandhu', or just 'East'.

It was strange. The youth of Europe was on the move, and until now Stephen had never known it.

'That's the one I'd take!' said Jerry, pointing to the last in the queue, a boy with long shiny hair sitting cross-legged on a mat with his eyes closed. 'That guy's got to be really into his own trip!'

Everybody else waved and smiled. Astrid smiled back down at them, and Jerry made a peace sign. It felt like being royalty.

They stopped briefly for Stephen to post his letter, and to telephone Thierry's mother and tell her in halting French that he wouldn't be coming, and then they drove.

Sitting on a stool behind the passenger seat, Stephen peered forward through the windscreen at a mellow, sunlit landscape of fields and little villages, with church spires, and trees just coming into bud.

So this was it. He was away. Free. On his way to Istanbul, to find his long-lost brother...

But even as he savoured the freedom, doubts began to form. It was all a bit too good to be true, wasn't it? What would his mother think, when she got his letter? She wouldn't approve, he knew that. She'd never believe he had a chance of finding Rob – a 'wild goose chase' she'd call it. She was always telling him not to trust strangers, and perhaps she was right; he really had no idea who these people were. They might change their minds and chuck him out anywhere. They might not be going to Istanbul at all. He should have gone to Thierry, and been safe, and left Rob to his own business . . .

On the road ahead, he made out a sign to Charleville – Thierry's home town, where he was supposed to be going.

Stephen felt a twinge of panic. This was his last chance; he could ask them to stop and let him out, and then he could hitchhike to Thierry's. He knew the address. That's what he should do.

He tapped Jerry on the shoulder.

'I think I should . . .'

Jerry turned round and grinned at him.

'Relax, man. We got a long way to go.'

Jerry put his feet on the dashboard and from somewhere under the seat pulled out a tobacco tin.

'It's just . . . that's the sign to Charleville. It's where I'm supposed to be going and . . .'

'Right. So you were,' said Jerry. 'Hey, maybe you'll still get to go there when you get back from Istanbul. You know what? I'm really glad you're with us. We're going to have a great time!'

Astrid was humming softly to herself, watching the road, not listening. The turn-off to Charleville sped past.

Stephen turned and watched through the back windows as the sign disappeared into the distance behind him. The back of the van was like a little home. There was a mattress with big velvet cushions, cupboards, and a cooker. There were no windows in the sides, just a sliding door. It was its own little world, and it felt safe. For better or for worse, he was here. He couldn't change his mind any more.

He glanced back towards Jerry, and then he stiffened. Jerry had opened his tin. In it he had some tobacco, cigarette papers and what looked like a lump of sandy earth. Stephen guessed immediately what it was. He'd read about it and talked about it, though he'd never seen it before.

Jerry was rolling a joint.

He laid a little mound of tobacco in the lid of the tin and put it ready on the dashboard. Then he flicked on his cigarette lighter and burnt an end of the lump. The smoke drifted towards Stephen, aromatic, sickly, seductive. Then Jerry crumbled the softened hashish into the palm of his hand.

Stephen's heart was racing again. So they were hippies after all. He should have listened to his mother. He should have known better. He glanced anxiously back through the window, but the turn-off to Charleville was long gone. If he was going to get out, he would have to do it at the next city, wherever that was, and take a train. If they let him... Perhaps they were kidnapping him, they were going to drug him and sell him into slavery. He'd read about something like that in the papers. Perhaps that was what happened to Rob.

Jerry turned and grinned at him. When he grinned, Jerry didn't look like a kidnapper.

'Hey, man, you smoke hash?' he shouted over the rumble of the motor.

'Not really,' said Stephen

'No, man, you're right at your age. Keep it pure. We're very into purity. You're too young to start on the dope. You don't need it. Eh, Astrid, he's too young, don't you think?'

Astrid turned quickly and beamed at Stephen.

'Too young? I don't think so. Too good, maybe.'

'It's good stuff though really,' continued Jerry. 'Opens the mind. When you're ready. Anyway, make yourself comfortable. We've got a lot of miles to cover.'

He finished rolling the joint, put his tin away, and settled his feet back up on the dashboard, inhaling deeply as the van sped along the empty road. He passed the joint to Astrid. She puffed a few times and handed it back. That was all, except for the steady rumble of the motor and the landscape flashing by.

Stephen's heart-rate slowed. It was all right. He wasn't scared of hashish, not really. All sorts of people smoked it. Even his English teacher didn't disapprove of it, and the stuff in the papers was all lies, everybody knew that. Nobody was going to force him to do anything he didn't want to. There was nothing for it, but to go with this adventure, and hope that Rob was at the end of it.

He took Jerry's advice, and moved to the mattress, lying back on the big velvet cushions. The smoke drifted into the back. He liked the smell of it. Hang Charleville, he thought. Thierry and his boring family could wait. Besides, Astrid was driving. She was leaning slightly forward over the steering wheel, focused and mysterious.

He could see the curve of her breast under her dress, and the turn of her nose, and the loose fall of her hair.

There was no going back.

He was fifteen. He could look after himself.

There was a poem the Wart had taught him. The Wart, otherwise known as Mr Wortle, was his English teacher, a man with a soft face and a love of poetry. Poems always stuck in Stephen's head. He didn't know why. He loved the delicate rhythms of them, and how you could say them over and over to yourself, always finding something new. That was why the Wart liked him, to begin with. This poem was called 'Byzantium'. That was Istanbul – the same place. He remembered some of it:

> *A starlit or a moonlit dome disdains*
> *All that man is,*
> *All mere complexities,*
> *The fury and the mire of human veins.*

Moonlit domes: that was better than two weeks with Thierry. Thierry had already been to stay with him. He was fussy about his food, and liked motorbikes, and wanted to be a policeman. He was all right. They hadn't argued, but they hadn't got on either. Thierry wouldn't understand about moonlit domes. And he'd have reported Jerry and Astrid to the nearest police station.

The hours passed, the sun set, and they sped on through the dark. Stephen lay against velvet cushions and dreamed of mosques and minarets and wide open starlit skies. Then, somewhere in Germany, Astrid pulled up and leant forward over the steering wheel, rubbing her eyes.

'We're stopping for the night. Astrid and I are going to take a room here,' Jerry called into the back. 'Do you mind sleeping in the bus? It's pretty comfortable.'

Stephen was happy to. He was half asleep already and felt at home there. He stretched out under some blankets, and slept soundly.

He woke when the van started, rubbing his eyes and trying to remember where he was as Jerry drove off, and Astrid turned round and smiled at him. She looked younger in the morning light, sitting upright with her legs tucked under her. The sun was just coming up, lighting up her hair.

'You sleep okay then, Stephen?'

'Yeah, fine.'

'Maybe you like some breakfast?'

She passed him a bag of pastries. Stephen picked one out. He could feel her watching him, with half a smile, as if she was measuring him up. He didn't know what to say.

'Thanks,' he managed.

'Don't mention it! Take two!'

He took another, grinning sheepishly. She smiled back, radiant.

They drove on, down through the middle of Europe. The first time they stopped to eat, Stephen offered to pay for himself, but he didn't have the right currency and Jerry brushed him aside.

'You're our guest, man.'

After that, Jerry paid. He seemed like a really kind, friendly guy. If Rob was living among people like this, no wonder he didn't want to come home.

They drove on, past fields and little woods and villages.

After a while, Astrid moved into the back and Stephen sat in the front next to Jerry. In the far distance they could just see a white line of mountains.

Jerry drummed his fingers on the steering wheel to a song he was hearing in his head, and Stephen thought about Rob.

He imagined seeing him again, the first meeting. Rob would be surprised at first, and then he'd smile, and then he'd give him a hug, and then they'd talk. Stephen would tell him all about . . .

About what? About Mum? About the greyness in her face and round her heart?

About Dad? But he could never talk to Rob about Dad. 'Why can't that zombie show some emotion, for a change?' Rob had said once, in the time when he still came home occasionally. Dad did have emotions, though. Stephen knew that, only too well. He just bottled them up because that's what he'd always had to do.

About Mr Wortle – the Wart? At the thought, Stephen felt something curl up inside him, and the blood rush to his face. Yet it was true, he might be able to tell Rob about the Wart. In fact Rob was probably the only person he could ever tell. Because Rob had been at Grindlesham too, and he knew what it was like. And Rob wouldn't go all moral. Rob wouldn't judge . . .

21

If it *was* Rob, and not some stranger who looked like him. And even if it was Rob, how might he have changed in a year and a half? Did he have a girlfriend? Would Jerry have mentioned that?

Stephen glanced over his shoulder at Astrid. She looked like a child, lying asleep. She wasn't as old as he had first thought – she was definitely younger than Jerry. She'd been so friendly, but what did she really think of him? He was just a kid to her, probably. Perhaps she'd had an affair with Rob. Perhaps they practised Free Love, like you read in the papers.

So many perhaps. He was travelling into the unknown, and he should have been afraid. But he wasn't.

He turned to Jerry.

'When did you last see Rob?' he asked.

'Rob? Let's think. It'd be a few months ago now. In Ibiza. We've got this really cool place there, like a community. Rob was part of it. He split a couple of months back, said he was heading East. That's where everybody's going now. Istanbul's just a great place.'

'You've been there before?'

'Yeah, a couple of times. I do a little business there.'

'What was Rob into?'

'Oh, music, writing songs and things, that kind of stuff... Oh, I know, I just remembered, last time I saw him, he was very into Rimbaud. You read any Rimbaud?'

'A bit,' said Stephen. At least he knew who Rimbaud was – a French boy poet from the nineteenth century who had amazed the literary world, and then given up

22

poetry to sell guns in Africa. Mr Wortle had talked about him and given Stephen one of his poems to read, and though he didn't fully understand it, he had liked its strangeness.

'I haven't,' Jerry admitted. 'I don't get to read that much, to be honest with you. I'm more into visual arts and music. But he sounded like one hell of a cat. Ran away from home at fifteen. Bit like you, huh?'

'I'm not running away,' said Stephen quickly. 'I'm going to find Rob.'

'Sure, yeah, of course. It was just a way of speaking. Anyway, this guy Rimbaud had this idea of totally deranging all his senses. He thought that was the way to become a prophet. He went to London with this other guy called Verlaine and they got really stoned.'

Stephen listened, waiting for something more, but it didn't follow.

'Anyway,' Jerry went on after a while, 'that's who Rob was into. Tell you what, though, I just read a fantastic book by Hermann Hesse. You heard of him? A guy gave me this book called *Journey to the East*. It really expressed something for me. That's what we're doing. This is our Journey to the East. I've got it in the back. You should read it.'

The Alps rose up huge in front of them, the snow-peaks glowing gold. Jerry finished a joint and wound down the window to push the stub out. A warm southerly wind blew into the cab.

Stephen felt a glow of excitement. He didn't care about the hashish – the only effect it had on Jerry and Astrid was to make them smile. They were glamorous, beautiful people, and he wanted to be with them. The world was opening up to him. The world was new.

Chapter 3

It was a long journey, far longer than Stephen had ever imagined.

At a roadside hotel, somewhere in Austria, Jerry asked Stephen to sleep in the bus again, but this time he couldn't get to sleep, because a dog kept barking. Then some men approached. The dog barked twice as fiercely, and the men shouted back at it. Eventually they went away. Stephen guessed they were drunk, but it unsettled him. He wondered if Jerry wanted him in the bus for security reasons.

The next day Astrid and Jerry were tense with each other, as if they had had a row. They sat silent in the front, and when they stopped for coffee in a cake shop in Vienna Astrid was distant and formal with Jerry, avoiding eye contact. She was extra friendly to Stephen, though, taking his hand and pretending to be a gypsy reading his palm and promising him long life and lots of beautiful wives. Stephen drank in the attention, while Jerry sucked his lip and drummed the table with his fingers.

And then Jerry drove on, right through the night. Astrid curled up like a cat in the back, while Stephen dozed uncomfortably in the front seat, using his coat for a pillow.

The morning sun lit up a different landscape, of rocky hillsides with cactus hedges, and poor, dusty villages where the children ran after the van, laughing and shouting. Astrid rubbed the sleep from her eyes and came and sat in the front – there was just about room for the three of them if they squeezed up.

They crossed the border into Greece, and at once the air seemed brighter and the wind warmer. Astrid rolled down her window and held her hand out into the breeze. Jerry grinned across at Stephen. His eyes were red from driving through the night, but his face was relaxed.

'Mediterranean, here we come!' he said.

A little further on, in the middle of nowhere, he stopped the van and got out to pee.

Astrid turned to Stephen and smiled. He smiled back. She held his gaze.

'You're really cute, you know that?'

Jerry got back in, rubbing his eyes. An hour later, they rounded a bend, and below them, beyond olive groves and orchards, stretched the blue line of the Mediterranean.

'Looks good, man,' said Jerry. 'Hey, what do you say? Let's find a village to stop off in, have ourselves a good meal and some retsina?'

It took longer than they expected, but when they found it, it was like paradise: a village of whitewashed houses, a taverna, waves lapping on the beach, and a purple sunset.

Jerry looked exhausted. He slumped over the steering wheel, and yawned.

A round woman dressed in black came out of the taverna.

'Allo!' she said. 'Yes, yes, you come here. You eat, sleep, no problem.'

She showed them some pleasant, simple rooms, and then they sat on the terrace drinking wine and eating moussaka and stuffed vine leaves and salads drenched in olive oil, brought by the landlady's son, Lefteris. After the road-side snacks of the journey, it tasted wonderful. The taverna was filling up with local people and a few early season tourists – four young backpackers and two middle-aged English ladies. Musicians arrived and tuned their instruments.

The moon had risen and was glittering over the Mediterranean, a few metres away.

Jerry's head was nodding.

'The wine's too much for me,' he said. 'I gotta crash! Coming, Astrid?'

'No,' she said. 'This is too nice. I stay a little bit with Stephen. Okay?'

Jerry looked surprised. Then he stood up, a little unsteady on his feet, from the wine or tiredness or both.

'Sure,' he said. 'That's cool. Enjoy yourselves.'

He rubbed his eyes and walked slowly round to the back where their rooms were.

Stephen had a room too. The woman had insisted; she'd looked at him closely and said firmly that he was not sleeping in the bus – not at her house. Jerry was too tired to argue.

For a moment, Stephen felt embarrassed to be sitting alone with Astrid. He was used to her now, the way she moved, the way she pushed back her hair, the way she smiled. She no longer seemed like a goddess. But she was still the loveliest girl he had ever met, and he could sense the envious glances of the backpackers and the admiring attentions of the Greek men.

But Astrid seemed to be oblivious to all that. Perhaps she took it for granted.

She played with an olive, taking tiny nibbles.

'How old are you, Stephen?' she asked.

'Sixteen.' It wasn't really a lie. He would be sixteen on his next birthday.

'Sixteen, and the world is new!'

'How old are you?' he asked. It seemed the natural thing to say.

She laughed.

'Never ask a woman her age! They always lie!' She took a sip of her wine. 'Nineteen. Does that seem ancient?'

'No,' said Stephen.

'It does to me, some days. You know, you look so like Rob.'

She smiled across at him, tipping her head on one side, and brushing her hair from her eyes with her hand in the way she had. Stephen felt his heart pounding.

'Does everyone call you Stephen? It sounds very formal.'

'Mostly... well, some of my friends call me Stevie...' or much ruder things, but he wasn't going to say that.

'Stevie, that's nice.'

The music suddenly seemed louder. People were dancing.

28

'Shall we dance, Stevie?'

He didn't know how to say no, and besides the wine was in his bloodstream, warming him and making him bold. Anyway, he loved dancing and knew he moved well. They stood up, and within seconds they were being shown the steps of the folk dance and were the centre of attention, with everyone laughing as they got it wrong. For a little while they got it right and were whirling round each other, Astrid's head thrown back in delight. When they finished, everyone clapped. They went back to their table and Lefteris brought them a special bottle of retsina, and a plate of octopus bits, and they smiled at each other and the rest of the taverna, flushed and happy.

The backpackers had packed up and gone. But the English ladies, on their third bottle of wine, waved at them approvingly.

They left the wine half drunk, and walked across the road to the beach.

Astrid was giggly and unsteady, and rubbed against Stephen as they walked.

They sat on a rock and listened to the swish of waves on the beach in front of them. The band was still playing in the taverna.

As he sat there, a picture flashed momentarily into Stephen's head, so vivid that he blinked. It was of his mother. Her face was grey and the wrinkles in her forehead were exaggerated as if by a harsh light. Her mouth was tight with disapproval. She was trying to say something, but her mouth wouldn't open properly.

His mother. She'd know by now that he hadn't gone to Thierry. What would she be doing? Would she have called the police? Or would she accept his letter, understand?

By his side, Astrid giggled and leant towards him.

His heart was pulsating. Instantly, he forgot all about his mother. He could feel Astrid's warmth and hear her breathing. Looking steadfastly out to sea, he lifted his arm and placed it on her shoulders.

He half expected her to push it off. But she laid her head against him and gave a deep sigh.

They sat there silently. Stephen hardly dared to move in case he broke the spell. There was a glow of fluorescence in the waves – or was it just the moonshine?

He felt Astrid's head move, and turned towards her. She straightened her back and met his eyes. Hers were huge in the moonlight.

She wasn't smiling. Her lips were apart.

Stephen felt he was melting, from deep in the stomach outwards. An erection was pressing against his jeans.

He put his other arm around her...

'Hey, you guys!'

Stephen started guiltily back, and Astrid stiffened.

It was Jerry, stumbling out to find them. He seemed to be still half asleep, more confused than anything.

He looked at them, trying to take it in.

'Oh, sorry,' he said. 'I was just wondering...I guess I woke up...'

'We were looking at the sea,' said Astrid. 'Stevie and I, we were looking at the sea.'

She stood up slowly, brushing her hand down Stephen's arm until he felt the touch of her fingertips on his. Then she went over to Jerry.

'Come on, I take you back to bed.'

She led him away.

She turned as she went, and gave Stephen a look.

The look seemed to say, 'Too bad!'

The next morning they set off again, on the last leg of the journey, heading for the Turkish border.

Chapter 4

'Hey, man, you going across? You give us a lift?'

Jerry leaned out of his window, but he looked doubtful. The boy he was talking to was not much older than Stephen, but his appearance was completely different. His hair was down over his shoulders, and his clothes were torn and filthy. His only luggage was an embroidered shoulder bag. Behind him stood a couple, both with long frizzy hair, both smiling hopefully, both with enormous rucksacks.

'I'd like to, but, hey, we're a bit full. Couldn't you just walk?'

'Walk? It's ten kilometres across the border. We've been waiting here an hour, man.'

It was true. They were at the Turkish border, and had gone through the Greek side with the merest formality, but it was several miles of barren road across to the Turkish side, with no public transport. If you hadn't got a vehicle you had to walk or get a lift.

'Come on, man, you got plenty of room in the back there.'

Jerry seemed reluctant.

'I'm not sure, man. I . . .'

From the back, Astrid interrupted him. She and Jerry had been arguing again, and she was short with him.

'Don't be stupid, Jerry. Of course we take them.'

She opened the back door and jumped out, and the

hitchhikers piled in with their luggage. She slid the door back shut, and opened the passenger door.

'I come in front with you, Stevie,' she said, smiling up at him.

Jerry raised his eyebrows and shrugged.

Stephen sat with Astrid pressed against him. He wanted to put his hand on her knee, but he didn't quite dare. She was friendly, but she had given little sign of the intimacy between them last night. Besides, he felt awkward with Jerry sitting next to them. Still, it was good to feel her body against his.

The three hitchhikers settled down amongst their luggage in the back. The couple with the enormous backpacks apparently spoke no English, but they smiled a lot.

They drove uphill through a barren landscape, the van struggling with the extra weight on the rutted road; Turkey and Greece had been at war only a few years before, and neither side was bothered about maintaining the road in this stretch of no-man's land.

They were driving into Turkey.

Tomorrow he would see Rob.

How long had it been? Since he saw Rob it was one year and seven months and a few days. Since he left England it had been – he had to count – four nights.

Four nights: another world.

A world of colour and constant change, where everything was new. Where no one said he was too young, or made fun of him. Where he was sitting next to the most beautiful girl on the planet.

As if she read his thoughts, at that moment Astrid looked round at him, met his eyes and smiled. Then she took his hand and squeezed it.

If the boys at school could see him... They wouldn't believe it. The thought of his school unsettled him for a moment, with sudden flashes of playing Rugby in the rain, and eating in the school dining hall, and Soames' face close up and leering at him. It all couldn't be further away, thank God. He'd never tell them, anyway. He'd never tell them about Astrid.

They were at the top of a hill. Below them, they could see the Turkish customs post. The Mediterranean was just visible in the distance. The bus picked up a bit of speed, relieved to be going downhill.

What would he say to Rob when he saw him?

There was so much. They'd have to talk through the night, at least. That is, if they had anything to say to each other at all. But of course they would... Only why had Rob gone silent? What if he didn't want to see Stephen? What if he just told him to go away? Surely he wouldn't do that, not when he'd come so far...

But he might. That was the thing about Rob. He might do anything.

Astrid squeezed his hand again, and leaned against his shoulder.

They rounded a corner, and there was the border post.

They were in Turkey.

'Get out!' said the guard. At least, that was the gist of it.

He said it in Turkish with accompanying gestures, while two or three others lounged behind him, all with revolver bulges on their hips. No one was inclined to misunderstand.

They filed into a dark office where a large man sat behind a wide desk with a Turkish flag. He was wearing a smart blue uniform with epaulettes, and had a heavy moustache; he reminded Stephen of a Mexican bandit from a cowboy movie. He didn't look up as they came in; one of the guards silently collected the passports and put them in a pile in front of him.

Eventually he finished the paper he was working on, put it aside, and started thumbing through the passports.

'You are all together?' he asked.

'No,' said Jerry. 'We just gave these guys a lift across the border.'

The man finally looked up. He stared at Jerry for a while, his features immobile.

'You know the penalties for possession of hashish in this country,' he said slowly. 'In Greece perhaps they are not so strict, but here we are not allowing it. If you are caught with it, you will go to prison for perhaps many years. If you are bringing some hashish or other drugs into this country then give it to me now. I am a kind man. We will say no more.'

He paused and looked at each of them in turn.

'We haven't got anything like that. We don't even smoke cigarettes,' said Jerry.

He said it too fast, Stephen thought. It didn't sound

convincing. Besides, he knew where the hash tin was, under the seat. They'd find it immediately if they looked. Why not hand it over? He shifted uneasily on his chair, wondering whether all of them would be sent to prison if they found it, or whether it would just be Jerry. But even that, how would he explain that to his mother?

The large man nodded his head gravely.

'Not smoking? I see,' he said. 'Then I won't offer you one of mine.'

His mouth twitched. It was supposed to be a joke. He took out a silver cigarette case, and lit an oval cigarette. He took his time.

'All the same, Turkish tobacco is very good. You should try it.'

The two hitchhikers with the big rucksacks were looking at each other. They had no idea what was going on.

The man made a dismissive gesture towards them.

'They can go!'

He stamped their passports; they grinned happily, and shouldered their rucksacks.

The large man turned his attention to the long-haired boy. He looked through his passport.

'Martin Jonke? You have done much travels, I see, Martin. For one so young. Open your bag!'

Martin put it on the table and opened it with a sullen look.

There was hardly anything in it – a thin sleeping bag; a grubby shirt and cotton trousers, a tin mug and a spoon, a wad of Drum tobacco and a packet of Rizla cigarette papers with the cardboard torn off.

The large man held up the Rizlas between forefinger and thumb.

'What's this for?'

'For roll-ups.'

'Where do you keep your money?'

'I have no money.'

'You have money. Where is it?'

Martin hesitated. The large man didn't. He gestured to one of the guards and said something in Turkish. The guard took Martin's arm.

'He will search you!'

Martin looked round helplessly as the guard led him to an adjoining room.

'It is better to do what you're told, don't you think, Mr...' The large man looked down at Jerry's passport. 'Mr Turnbull.'

'Absolutely,' agreed Jerry, confidently. Too confidently, Stephen thought.

'Ye...es, well let me see, this is your vehicle, yes, registered in your name?'

'Yes.'

'The papers are in order, I hope...'

They waited silently while he read them through. He took his time over it, then put them aside, and looked at Astrid.

'This is your wife?'

Astrid stared at her knees and said nothing.

'No,' said Jerry. 'Not yet anyway.'

37

'Hmm.' The large man picked up her passport and glanced at it without much interest.

'And the young gentleman?'

He emphasised the word 'young', looking hard at Stephen as he thumbed through his passport. Stephen tried to look away but it was impossible not to meet those big dark eyes, or to see the way his lips parted and his tongue clicked against his upper teeth.

'Your first visit to Turkey, I see. I hope you will enjoy our country.'

The door to the adjoining room opened, and the guard came back. He spoke briefly and placed some items on the desk in front of the large man.

There was a wad of dollar bills in a rubber band, a penknife and a small piece of hash.

The large man threw his head back and laughed.

'In his shoe!' he said between guffaws. 'He hid it in his shoe! He thought he was so clever.'

The laughter stopped as suddenly as it began.

'Take him away! We will deal with him later.'

He stood up.

'I think we had better have a look in your car, don't you, Mr Turnbull?'

Jerry shrugged.

'If you want,' he said.

There were five guards; they took out whatever they could and laid it in the dust at the roadside: Stephen's suitcase, Astrid's clothes packed in a basket, Jerry's camera and guitar, unused cooking pots and jars of spices. Then they searched the car, looking behind the woodwork, tapping against the tyres.

The large man watched, smoking.

Jerry and Astrid stood together, saying nothing.

The guards were working from the back to the front. Stephen put the contents of his suitcase back together, wondering when they'd get to look under the front seats. Already one of them was nosing about in the cab.

Then, quite suddenly, the large man stubbed out his cigarette, and walked back to his office.

'That will do! You can go!' he announced.

They followed him back inside. He stamped their passports and handed them over.

As Stephen took his, the large man held onto it for a second, leaning forward and smiling heavily.

'Welcome to our country. I wish you happy stay.'

Night was falling as they approached the city. Oncoming lorries screeched past flashing their lights, as they drove through a landscape of cement factories and slum housing.

Stephen lay in the back of the bus, feeling sleepy. In the front, Astrid and Jerry were arguing again. He couldn't hear what it was about over the sound of the motor, and he didn't care either.

He was going to see Rob. He had to keep telling himself: he was going to see Rob. Because part of him still didn't believe it. The journey seemed to have separated him from his past. His home, his school – Thierry, his mother, Mr Wortle – they all seemed lost and far away, belonging to another reality, as if all the things that had happened to him in the past had happened to somebody else. Did Rob belong in that past, or was he part of this new world – the future? Or was he neither, lost in a limbo in between?

Late in the night they arrived at the Oteli Fivestar, a hotel in the centre of Istanbul, with a locked parking area and a thin-faced manager, who welcomed Jerry and Astrid as old friends. He showed them to rooms on the first floor, where Stephen collapsed onto his bed and fell into a deep sleep.

He woke with the dawn, still in his clothes. He got up, went over to the window and opened it. The morning air was fresh and pleasant, but a concrete block of flats cut out most of the view.

Then he heard it. It was a sound he had never heard before, though he had read about it, and knew immediately what it was. Cutting across the hum of traffic, and distorted by amplification, it nonetheless made his spine tingle: the morning call to prayer.

Allahu akbar, Allahu akbar, Allahu akbar.

Was it his imagination, or had the roar of the traffic lessened, as if the whole city was pausing for a moment to welcome the new day by kneeling in prayer?

Ashadu an la illaha ill'allah.

40

It was only sound to him. He would have liked to know what it meant.

He went downstairs. There was nobody at the reception, but the front door was open. He went out into the street, which was narrow and quiet. Down one end he could see and hear the traffic on a big road; at the other end, up the hill, were trees.

He walked towards the trees, and came out into a big open park.

In front of him was an enormous mosque, reflected in the waters of an ornamental lake. He knew this must be the Blue Mosque. Its six minarets caught the first rays of the sun rising over Asia, but the domes were still shrouded in shadow.

He stood amazed, drinking it in.

A starlit or a moonlit dome disdains
All that man is,
All mere complexities . . .

Only it didn't need to be starlit or moonlit.

He sat on a bench to watch the light changing, while birds chattered in the trees above him. People were crowding out of the mosque, men and women separately, their prayers finished, going to start their businesses. No one took any notice of him. Everything was different here, different from anything he had experienced before – the light, the colours, the people and above all this enormous mosque, its domes and minarets hovering above the gardens, pointing to another realm.

★

41

Back at the Oteli Fivestar, the manager was behind his desk, and nodded to him as he came in. He lingered outside Jerry and Astrid's room for a moment. He could hear them talking, and thought of knocking, but decided against it. He didn't want to interrupt anything. His own room was further down the corridor, so he left his door ajar, so that he would hear them when they came out, and then he could go and have breakfast with them – Jerry would know where to go.

He sat on his bed for a moment, thinking about Astrid. She was Jerry's girl, he knew that. They argued a lot, but they were still a couple. It couldn't come to anything with her... Or could it? She did like him, he was sure. Perhaps she *really* liked him. He could still feel the tingle, when she had taken his hand. Yet when he wasn't with her she still seemed unreal, like a fantasy.

He opened his suitcase. All his clothes were dirty, at least all that he wanted to wear. He couldn't see himself putting on his best shirt with the stiff collar, or the Sunday suit that his mother had insisted on him taking. All his other shirts, socks and underwear were filthy. So were the jeans that he'd been wearing every day, though they didn't show it so much. He wondered if he could find a laundry. He had no idea how to get things done... but Jerry, or Rob, or somebody would tell him. Otherwise it would have to wait till he got back to his mother.

He heard a sound and turned.

Astrid was in the doorway, watching him. She was wearing her Moroccan dress and carrying two baskets, one on each shoulder. She had been crying. As soon as he turned, she came in quickly, putting down her baskets and shutting the door behind her.

She stood there, staring at him, with her eyes wide and her cheeks tear-stained, shaking slightly as if she was in shock.

'I have to go,' she said. 'I come to say goodbye.'

Stephen was crouched on the floor, his mouth hanging open foolishly, not knowing what to do or say.

'What do you mean? Why...?' he managed.

He stood up. Behind him the contents of his suitcase were spilling out over the floor. Astrid ran to him and put her arms around his neck and hugged him. He could feel her breasts pressing against his chest.

'I am sorry,' she said. 'I just have to go. I can't stay with Jerry, and I can't stay here without him. I am afraid for what he is doing. I can't explain. I am worried about you, too, after we brought you here. You will be all right, yes? You will find your brother... you will find Rob... He is here, I am sure... I hope...'

She buried her head in his shoulder and started to sob, then stopped herself. She broke away and wiped her tears.

'Oh, Stevie!'

She held his hand and looked deep into his eyes.

'I see you one day again, Stevie. I know it!'

She kissed him, a real kiss, full on the mouth. Then before he had properly taken in what was happening, she broke away from him and was gone.

★

43

Jerry was sitting on his bed practising chords on his guitar.

He nodded to Stephen to sit on the other bed – the one that had been Astrid's until a few minutes before. He seemed unconcerned.

'What's happened with Astrid?' Stephen asked.

Jerry shrugged and grinned.

'Chicks, huh? She freaked out. It's a thing that's been going on for a while. She's left.'

'Where to?'

'Back to her father's in Germany. We had a bit of a row, but don't worry, it was sort of semi-planned anyway. She's got an airline ticket. I'll see her again in a few weeks, I guess. I have a bit of business to do here first. And we've got to find your brother.'

He put down his guitar.

'Hey, Stephen, it's not because of anything to do with you – you know that? She just split. Don't worry about it. I'm still here, right? We're friends, right?'

He met Stephen's eyes and grinned. Stephen grinned back. He couldn't help it.

He suddenly felt bad that he had flirted with Astrid. It must have hurt Jerry, though he was too cool to show it, and Jerry was his friend.

'I'm ready for breakfast,' said Jerry. 'Come on, I'll show you Istanbul.'

Chapter 5

'I wanted to ask you something,' said Stephen. 'You know when we were at the border and they were searching the van. Weren't you worried they'd find your hash tin?'

Jerry laughed.

'Man, you've got to be pretty stupid to bring hash from Greece to Turkey. For one thing that guy at the customs is a real bastard, and for the other hash is much cheaper in Turkey. No, I never take anything through that border. I ditched the hash before we got there. Pity though in a way. I've got nothing to smoke now. That guy, though, Martin. Hope he's all right. They could put him in prison for that.'

They were in the Pudding Shop, a famous hippy meeting place in Istanbul. As they walked in, Stephen half expected to see Rob, sitting among the long-haired, loose-clothed travellers. But it was early, and still half empty. There was a big notice board all along one wall, covered with messages that ranged from the practical – *Australian woman seeks ride to India* – to the personal – *Hey, Babs, I love you! Meet me here Wednesday at sunset* – to the surreal: *The drunken boat lives!* accompanied by swirling crayon artwork. Letters were pinned up too. Stephen examined them carefully, but there was nothing for, to, or about Rob. On Jerry's prompting he wrote a notice himself and pinned it up:

Rob

— are you out there, in the bee-loud glade?

Stevie

'What does that mean. "Bee-loud glade?"' asked Jerry.

'It's a sort of private joke,' said Stephen. 'It's from a poem, about living on an island and growing beans and keeping bees. Rob used to read it to me. It's so he'll know it's me.'

'Far out!' said Jerry.

The Pudding Shop sold Turkish coffee and sweet black tea in glasses, and of course puddings — Turkish confections of pastry and honey, and milk puddings similar to blancmange. It was remarkably clean, with a glass cabinet for the puddings, and plastic table tops. It also had one of the few tape recorders in Istanbul, with a stack of tapes left by travellers.

Jerry drummed his fingers on the table to the music.

'You dig the Doors?'

Stephen had never heard of them. He'd never listened to music all that much; that was Rob's thing. He knew the Beatles and the Rolling Stones, and he knew what was top of the hit parade, but he'd never heard music like this, sweet and harsh and insistent and unhurried all at the same time. Music from another world. He sipped his tea and listened.

When the music's over. . .

Turn out the light!

A tall man with long wild hair and a goatee beard came through the door. He looked over their way, and then stopped and did a big double take.

'Hey, Jerry, man, what ya doin'?'

Jerry stood up grinning.

'Reuben! Hi, man! Good to see you.'

They hugged, and Reuben sat down with them.

'Hey, I was wondering when you'd turn up here, Jerry, man. You just got in? Astrid with you?'

'She was. She split this morning.'

'Too bad, huh. Who's this guy?'

He looked at Stephen with an air of disapproval. Stephen felt suddenly aware of his conventional clothes and short hair.

'Oh yeah, this is Stephen. You remember Rob, who hung out with us in Spain? He's his brother.'

'Too much!' said Reuben. He looked again at Stephen, this time raising an eyebrow with a nod of approval – being Rob's brother obviously made him acceptable. 'Rob's kid brother? I should have guessed. You're the spittin' image of him, now I come to look at you . . . Just add a bit of hair and funky clothes!'

'Have you seen Rob?' asked Jerry. 'We're looking for him.'

'No, man, not for a week or two. But he was here. He was definitely here. I ran into him in this very place and scored some hash off him. Hey, you got anything, you know, like . . . ?'

Jerry shrugged.

'Not at this moment. Try me in a few days.'

'Too bad. Well, I gotta split right now, but I'll see you guys later, right?'

'There you are,' said Jerry, as Reuben left. 'He's seen Rob. We'll find him easy. He might come in at any moment.'

He might. And then again he might not. 'A week or two' could mean anything. Rob could be back in England by now, for all Stephen knew. Yet Reuben definitely knew Rob, and that was something. If Rob did suddenly turn up, though, Stephen was sure he didn't want to meet him looking the way he did.

'Jerry,' said Stephen. 'Do you think you could help me get some, well, more comfortable clothes?'

Jerry laughed.

'Great idea! let's check out the bazaar, and see what we can do.'

It was all bewildering at first, as they entered the maze of small streets that led to the covered bazaar. Stephen stuck close to Jerry, who pushed his way determinedly through the crowds. Ragged, bright-eyed boys pulled at his clothes, demanding baksheesh or trying to sell trinkets or single cigarettes from packets of Marlboroughs. The noise of traffic on the main road gave way to a babble of voices arguing, talking, shouting their wares. An electric shop blared out badly amplified music. The men looked like Chicago gangsters with heavy moustaches and double-breasted brown suits. Women pulled their headscarves across their mouths to act as veils. Everybody stared at him. And there was an intensity of smells such as he had never before experienced: spices and incense and sweetmeats and hot oil and garlic and human sweat and bad plumbing, all mixing and mingling.

It was all new, and he loved it.

They went through a gateway with a golden crest above it, and he found himself in the ancient covered bazaar.

Stephen blinked. It was darker here, and quieter, and he recognised the atmosphere. It was the world of the Arabian Nights, of fat merchants and thieves and beautiful women on secret assignments. It was the East. He walked entranced through the labyrinth of walkways.

'Come on, man!' said Jerry. 'You can lose yourself here later. We'll sort you some clothes first.'

Jerry led him to an alley of clothes shops, and Stephen was soon enjoying himself, trying on loose cotton trousers and embroidered waistcoats.

Jerry watched admiringly.

'Hey, that looks cool. You should get some sandals too.'

'I'm getting a bit short of money,' said Stephen. 'I hope I've still got enough for a train ticket.'

Jerry put an arm on his shoulder.

'No worries, man. I'll see you straight. You can pay me back next time I'm in England.'

Stephen looked round at him. Jerry was grinning. He was his friend now, Stephen thought. His friend – all the more so now that Astrid had gone. And what a nice guy, really. He didn't know where Jerry came from, or how he made a living, but it wasn't important. He was a world away from those kind of superficialities. Openness and trust were what counted, and he knew he could trust

Jerry. Even if he didn't find Rob, Jerry would look after him.

He felt great in his new clothes. They left the bazaar, and checked out a few cafés for Rob, with no success, then walked down to the sea, where they bought freshly grilled fish from a stall, and looked across the narrow stretch of water to Asia.

Asia! Stephen gazed across at it with a strange longing, as if something was pulling him onwards, to see the next thing, and the next, and then the next, in this extraordinary world. Perhaps he could make a day trip with the ferry, just to have been there.

'Have you been across?' he asked Jerry.

'Not yet,' said Jerry. 'But a lot of guys are doing it now. You just keep on going and you get right on through to India. I always wanted to go to Benares myself, I don't know why. Something about the Ganges, I guess. When I'm ready, I'll make the journey.'

Little waves splashed against the rocks, and the sun was hot on Stephen's head. A cat watched them acutely from a pile of rubbish. He felt a deep contentment. There didn't seem much chance of finding Rob here any more. Stephen had almost given up on that. Even if Rob had been here once, he had gone; he might even be back in England. But it didn't matter, because Stephen had found something else, something that was for him: Astrid's head on his shoulders; this light on the Bosphorus; the Blue Mosque in the dawn.

Rob was out there somewhere, living with a fullness that Stephen could not have imagined up till now – that was Rob's business. He was not his brother's keeper. Tomorrow or the next day, Stephen would go back home on the Orient Express, but all this would remain, and for him, knowing that, nothing would ever be the same. Like Jerry, when he was ready he would return for it.

'I've got to go and meet someone about some business,' said Jerry, throwing the remains of his fish to the cat. 'I'll see you back at the hotel later.'

'Fine,' said Stephen dreamily. 'I'll check out the trains.'

It was evening when Jerry got back. He came to Stephen's room and sat on the edge of his bed. He seemed jumpy, sucking at his lip as he had done sometimes on the road.

'You check the trains then?' he asked.

'Yes, I managed to find someone who spoke English. The Orient Express leaves at 8 o'clock in the evening, twice a week. The next one's tomorrow.'

'You buy a ticket then?'

'No, I didn't have the cash with me. I'm a bit worried about the hotel bill actually. Do you know how much it'll be? I think I've got enough otherwise, if I change the rest of my traveller's cheques. I'll do it tomorrow.'

Jerry grinned.

'No worries, man! I bet we run into Rob this evening, and anyway I'll lend you some money, so you can enjoy yourself. Pick up a few more nice clothes, why not? They cost nothing here, compared with in England. And don't worry about the hotel, I'll pay that. Hey, I finally got something to smoke today. Mind if I . . . ?'

51

He pulled out his tin.

'Is it safe?' asked Stephen.

'Sure,' said Jerry. 'Some hotels get busted pretty regular, but this one's fine.'

He started to roll his joint.

'You know what, you remember that guy who sells nuts down the road? They taste really beautiful. Do you think you could go and get us a packet? Or two maybe.'

For a moment Stephen resented Jerry sending him off like a servant. But he didn't mind really. He enjoyed being out and part of this bustling city. He bought two packets of freshly roasted hazelnuts from the crippled vendor, who perched from dawn to dusk at the edge of the pavement where the taxis raced down the hill, and smiled at him as if he was an old friend. The nuts were delicious and Stephen ate half of them on the way back.

He was gone for ten minutes.

Reuben was in the Pudding Shop again that evening, already sitting there when they came in. He beckoned them over, nodding approvingly at Stephen's new clothes.

'You're coming on, kid.'

There was a girl sitting with him.

'This is Janey, man. She's really cool.'

She was slim and pretty with a wide mouth, but with a toughness around her eyes. She wore an embroidered skull cap and a long dress. She looked curiously at Stephen.

'She's just come overland, all the way from Australia. Man, she's got some stories.'

They sat down.

'Sorry,' said Janey, packing a notebook into her bag. 'I've got to go. I'm meeting somebody.'

'How ya doin'?' Reuben asked Jerry.

'Yeah, great,' said Jerry. 'It's good to be here. No sign of Rob yet, though. You haven't seen him?'

Reuben shook his head.

'No man, now I come to think of it, I reckon he must've split a couple of weeks back. I haven't seen him since then, and I've been around.'

'Rob?' asked Janey suddenly. 'You're looking for a guy called Rob? English guy?'

'Yeah,' said Jerry. 'He's Stephen's brother and we were hoping to run into him here.'

Janey looked at Stephen again.

'Bit of a crazy guy? Looks like you, but with long hair, and a bit older?'

Stephen shrugged. He really didn't know how Rob might look by now, but Janey took it as agreement.

'I knew him in Afghanistan.'

'Wow,' said Jerry. 'How's that, man? I told you we'd find him.'

Stephen's heart was beating fast. There was something about the intensity of this girl that made him think she *had* seen Rob, and recently. Yet he felt a disappointment too.

'But he's not here,' he pointed out.

'Well, no,' said Jerry. 'But he's in Afghanistan. So now you know where he is, for sure. Small world, huh?'

'He was there when I left ten days ago,' said Janey. 'If it's the same guy. But I'm sure he is. You look just like him. I saw it immediately.'

She smiled at Stephen, a broad smile with uneven teeth, keeping her eyes on him and ignoring the other two. Stephen warmed to her, wondering what she had to do with Rob, what had passed between them?

'How was he? Was he okay?' he asked.

'Oh, don't worry, Rob's fine. Crazy guy, but he can look after himself. You really are his brother, aren't you . . .'

She stood up and came round beside him, squatting down next to his chair, and talking softly as if she wanted only him to hear.

'Listen: Rob knows what he is doing, but he's on his own trip, and it's not an easy one, not for him, not for anybody. It's a long way to Afghanistan. It's a beautiful country, but it is a hard and dangerous country, and that's how Rob is too. I'd let him go if I were you . . . Well, who am I to say? It could be amazing. But if you're not ready, go home. It's cool.'

She stood up and smiled at him.

'Maybe I'll catch you later. If not, look after yourself. Cheers, Reuben.'

She left.

'Afghanistan, huh?' said Jerry.

Afghanistan. The word resonated in Stephen's brain. Afghanistan. It was only a name to him. He hadn't much idea where it was. He wished he'd paid more attention in

Geography at school, but they probably didn't teach about it anyway, not if it wasn't one of the red bits on the globe that used to be the British Empire. He should try and find a map somewhere, and look it up. Afghanistan . . . Afghanistan . . . Somewhere impossibly remote. A place of mountains and desert, of starlit mosques and ruined caravanserais. Somewhere beyond the boundaries of normal time and space. Somewhere where his home could never reach him.

'Afghanistan,' echoed Reuben. 'Sounds like quite a place to hang out. The dope's almost free and the people are cool. Spacey scenery, too. I'd like to go there myself.'

'Me too,' said Jerry.

Chapter 6

It took Stephen a long time to get to sleep that night. The elation he had felt for most of the day had dissolved, leaving a vague feeling of worry.

There was so much to take in, so much that was completely new. What had happened to Astrid, for a start, to make her run off like that? Just some tiff with Jerry, probably. Unless it was about him. It seemed incredible, but she really did like him, he was sure of that.

'I see you one day again, Stevie. I know it,' she had said as she kissed him.

Perhaps she would, though he couldn't see how. But then he hadn't foreseen any of what had happened to him in the last few days. Life, as his mother never tired of saying, was full of surprises.

The memory of the kiss awoke his desire, but he was too tired for that now. She was gone and he'd miss her: the most beautiful girl in the world, that was all.

How long had he been away from home? Stephen counted the days: this would be his sixth night. Less than a week. It didn't feel like a week. It felt like forever.

He thought about his parents. They'd be worried. He hoped they hadn't reported him missing or anything. Perhaps he should send them a telegram. But what would he say? He hadn't found Rob, that was the point. He'd found people who knew him and he was sure he was still alive, but he hadn't found him. His mother, he knew, would not believe him. He could see her face...

There was nothing he could do. He'd send a telegram in the morning, and then maybe he could stay here a couple of days longer, if Jerry lent him some money. It was too late to go to Thierry now anyway, and there was another ten days till school started.

School! And that meant... No, he wouldn't go into that. He pushed it out of his consciousness. After all, he was here: Istanbul. The image of the Blue Mosque floated into his mind, its domes reflecting the sunlight, hovering like another realm, aspired to but never quite realised in this hyperactive city with its blaring yellow taxis and cats fighting outside the restaurants, its smell of diesel and incense and rotting rubbish, the jasmine in the gardens, the crippled nut vendor, all the beauty and desperation of commerce – the fury and the mire – and then the sudden unexpected pools of delight: the Blue Mosque... the minarets... the call to prayer. He drifted off to sleep.

He woke suddenly. There were lights and shouting in the corridor, then a banging at his door. Blearily he got out of bed in his pyjamas and opened it. A policeman was standing there. There were others behind him, knocking on all the doors. The hotel seemed to be full of them.

'What's the matter? What's happening?' asked Stephen.

The policeman looked at him, and said something in Turkish, then pushed him aside and looked quickly round the room. It was a cursory inspection. He flicked over the mattress and glanced in the suitcase, but he obviously wasn't expecting to find anything.

He grinned at Stephen as he left.

'Okay, no problem. Have good stay in our country.'

Stephen got dressed. They were still shouting in the corridor – they must have woken the whole hotel. He wondered what they were looking for; drugs probably.

Then he thought of Jerry. Jerry had bought hash yesterday, he knew that. They'd catch him, they'd be sure to. Perhaps it was him they were after.

He opened his door again, so that he could see out into the corridor. Jerry's room was two doors away, and it seemed to be full of policemen shouting.

He felt an upsurge of panic. They were going to arrest Jerry, he knew it. Jerry was a drug smuggler. Suddenly that was obvious. But he was Stephen's friend too. He'd been good to him, looked after him, was going to lend him money... He had to know what was happening, whether Jerry would be all right.

He stepped out into the corridor, and as he did so, two policemen came out of Jerry's room, leading Jerry between them. A third followed just behind. The manager of the hotel stood obsequiously by.

'What's happening?' said Stephen. 'What's going on?'

'It's all right, man,' said Jerry. 'I think they got the wrong guy. We'll clear it up at the police station.'

The policeman standing behind him looked at Stephen suspiciously.

'This your friend?' he asked.

'No,' said Jerry. 'We just saw each other in the corridor here this afternoon. That's all.'

The policeman looked closely at Stephen.

'You are this man's friend. You come with him.' It was a statement, not a question.

For a moment Stephen wanted to say, yes, Jerry was his friend, and that he'd stick by him. But something in Jerry's face told him not to, that Jerry would rather he didn't.

'No,' he said, blushing and looking down. 'No, it's like he said. I just wanted to know what was going on...'

They waited. The manager shifted from foot to foot saying nothing. The policeman stepped forward till he was right opposite Stephen. He was a tall man, with an intelligent face. He put a finger under Stephen's chin and tilted it up towards him, looking closely in his eyes. Stephen knew that he knew that he was lying.

And then something softened in him. Perhaps he had children Stephen's age himself.

'Well,' he said. 'You are very young. Go back to bed now.'

Stephen went into his room and closed the door. He heard them taking Jerry down the stairs. For a little while longer, doors continued to bang, and voices to shout, then the hotel went quiet again.

He slumped on his bed, wondering what to do.

Jerry was in bad trouble, Stephen knew that. The police had probably come there specially to find him. They might have had a tip-off. God knows how much hash he had, hidden in his bag or even in the van. They'd be sure to have found it. He could go to prison for a long time for that. He was touched that Jerry had been so keen not to implicate him; that was really thoughtful.

He realised he was shaking. It had been more of a shock than he thought.

He counted his money again. There was enough for his train ticket, but not if he had to pay the hotel bill. Somehow, he didn't think Jerry had paid it. Perhaps he could sell something, to make the money up. Yesterday in the bazaar, someone had wanted to buy his watch, but he couldn't sell that, because it had been his grandfather's. He looked at his suitcase. It was a birthday present from his mother, and it was good quality, but it was too bulky and heavy for him now, and he'd rather have a rucksack. It would be worth something, but, when he thought about it, probably not enough.

He picked up his passport and flicked through it. Inside the front cover was written in florid italics:

Her Britannic Majesty's Principal Secretary of State for Foreign Affairs Requests and requires in the Name of Her Majesty all those whom it may concern to allow the bearer to pass freely without let or hindrance, and to afford the bearer such assistance and protection as may be necessary.

'Such assistance and protection as may be necessary...' That was it then. He was a British citizen. He could keep his suitcase, because the Embassy would help him out. He would go there in the morning, and they would get him a ticket for the Orient Express in the evening. That was what they were there for.

The first light of dawn was just perceptible outside his window, and the birds had started singing. How could there be so many birds in such a dirty city, he wondered as he fell asleep.

When he woke he could hear from the traffic that the day was well advanced. With a shudder, he remembered the events of the night before – poor old Jerry, locked up in some cell somewhere – then washed quickly and got ready to go out. He had to find the British Embassy, but first he needed some breakfast.

As he went through the lobby, the manager was waiting for him at the desk.

'You are leaving today?'

'I might do,' said Stephen.

'Better you leave,' said the manager. 'You pay now, please.'

'Couldn't I have my breakfast first?' asked Stephen.

'You pay now please. Also you pay bill for your friend.'

'My friend?'

'Mr Jerry. He is your friend. Please don't forget I know that. He has left last night with not paying his bill.'

'What about the van?' asked Stephen. 'He's left that here. It's got a lot of valuables in it.'

'Van has also been taken by police, for searching. Who knows what they find? You pay bill, please.'

'I don't have enough lire,' said Stephen truthfully. 'I'll have to go to the bank first.'

The manager shook his head. He clearly thought that once out of the building, Stephen might never be seen again.

'You have traveller cheque? Dollar? Sterling?'

Stephen nodded.

'Sterling.'

'Then pay with traveller cheque.'

He signed a cheque. The manager gave him some change in Turkish lire, but paying for both rooms cost a lot of money. He had two traveller's cheques left now, for £10 each, plus some French francs and two pound notes. It wouldn't last him very long.

'I'm probably taking the Orient Express this evening,' he said. 'Can I leave my bag in the room for the day?'

'Checkout is 12.00 noon,' said the manager, turning away.

He didn't go to the Pudding Shop, because he didn't want to meet Reuben and have to tell him about Jerry. Not yet, anyway. He found a quieter place round the corner and ordered tea and bread and jam. He was getting a taste for black Turkish tea, sucking it through sugar lumps, as he had seen the locals do it.

A girl wanted to sit at his table, because there were no others free. He gestured her to sit down, hardly noticing her. He was thinking about his home, wondering just how angry his mother would be. Should he send a telegram to say he was coming, or just turn up? At least his father would be on his side...

'You're English, aren't you?' asked the girl.

'Yes,' he said. 'How did you guess?'

'I can always tell,' she said. 'English, French, German, American. Americans stick out a mile. They seem bigger than everybody else, even when they're small. They can't help it.'

'Where are you from?'

'I'm Irish,' she said.

'I wouldn't have guessed it.'

'No,' she said. 'I try not to be too obvious. It's a matter of survival.'

Stephen looked at her properly. It was true, she was remarkably hard to see. She had a scarf over her hair like the local women wore, and loose clothes that gave her a hippyish look but would also have blended easily into a Turkish crowd. Her face was pleasant and unremarkable, and now that he looked closely he could see that she was not much older than he was.

'So what's your story?' she asked. 'What's brought you to Istanbul?'

He told her about Rob, and about Jerry, and about the bust and the hotel bill and his lack of money. It was a relief to tell it to someone, and she was easy to talk to. His story just flowed out, and she smiled with her eyes, and made sympathetic noises.

'I'm going to the Embassy now,' he said. 'See if they can help. I suppose I'll have to lug that suitcase with me...'

The girl looked doubtful.

'It's not an Embassy, just a Consulate, and you might be

lucky, but I've heard most of them are pretty useless. These days, they're only interested in businessmen. They look down their noses at you and tell you it's all your fault anyway. But you can leave your bag in our hotel if you like – the manager does a left luggage service.'

They left the café together, and she walked with him to the Oteli Fivestar.

'By the way, my name's Mary.'

'I'm Stephen. Are you on your own here?'

'Well, I've got a boyfriend, but he's useless. I thought he might be some good, because he's older than me, but he's not. He just lies around stoned all day and I have to sort everything.'

Stephen packed his suitcase quickly, shoving his clothes in any old how. They were all dirty anyway.

'The hotels do laundry services, you know,' Mary pointed out helpfully. 'And the *hamams* are great for a bath. But I suppose you'll get your mum to do all that for you now, when you get home.'

She took him to her hotel. It was called Oteli Gulhane.

'It's a bit crazy,' said Mary. 'Lots of weirdos and junkies. But it's cheap. Three lire a night to sleep in the Tent.'

'The Tent?'

'You haven't heard of the Tent? I thought everyone knew about it. It's a corrugated iron shack on the roof. You can buy floor space to put down your sleeping bag. It's the cheapest place to stay in Istanbul.'

'Are you short of money too, then?' asked Stephen.

Mary dropped her voice.

'Don't tell anyone – I've got a bit, but I'm trying to hang onto it. I want to go East. Afghanistan. India, maybe – if only I could get Brian to move out of his sleeping bag for five minutes.'

The manager of the Oteli Gulhane admired Stephen's suitcase as he put it in the locked room behind the reception desk.

'If you want sell, you ask me first,' he said. 'I give best price. Also, why not you stay some days this hotel? We have very nice room for you. Cheapest and best.'

'Thanks,' said Stephen. ' But I'm leaving tonight.'

'See you later,' said Mary. 'Look up and say hello when you pick up the bag, won't you?'

'I will,' said Stephen. 'And thanks!'

He changed the rest of his money at a bank.

Then he hailed a taxi and asked for the British Consulate.

He might as well spend the money he had. He was going home.

Chapter 7

It was only a twenty-minute taxi drive, but it was a journey to a different world – a twentieth-century world of high rise offices, where fashionable women dressed in short skirts and men wore ties and dealt in finance.

Suddenly Stephen felt dirty. He wished he had worn his suit rather than the clothes he had bought with Jerry, which were already grimy and made him look like a hippy.

The consulate was on the fifth floor of an office block. He went up in an elevator.

He knew he would have to wait to see the consul, so he had brought a book with him. It was the one Jerry had lent him: *Journey to the East*. He would never be able to return it now, so he would keep it to remind himself of Jerry and Astrid, and this strange journey to the East that they had brought him on.

He leafed through it, but he couldn't concentrate. He kept thinking about Rob, wondering what he was doing in Afghanistan, whether he had a girlfriend, how he managed for money. Yesterday he thought he had let go of Rob, but he realised now that he hadn't, that he missed him more than ever. 'Crazy', that was how Janey had described him, and he was, he always had been, while Stephen was the plodder, the good boy who never had the same brilliance, never won the prizes.

It took quite a lot to be expelled from Grindlesham. Rob managed it by shooting at the prefects in the school quadrangle with an air rifle. He had hung out of an upstairs window, laughing as they jumped and skipped to avoid the slugs.

'I didn't want to hit them,' he explained to Stephen later. 'It was just great seeing them dance.'

And then the school had him back, because of the prizes he won, because they expected him to get a scholarship to Oxford – and possibly because his mother had pleaded with them.

It didn't make any difference. Rob left anyway of his own accord, before he had taken his A-levels.

For a moment, Stephen wondered why he wanted to see Rob. Rob was charming and funny, but he could be a pain, and there had been nothing but rows when he was at home. At least things were quiet now.

But that wasn't the point, because Rob wasn't coming back home anyway. He never would now. It was just the hole that he'd left, the hole of not knowing. That's why Stephen had had to look for him.

He needed to justify it, though, to himself if nobody else. Somebody had left a pencil on the table, and he picked it up and noted on the inside cover of *Journey to the East*:

Reasons for trying to find Rob:

1. the hole inside

2. to talk about home

Yes, that was important, because Rob had always been the person he shared that with. A brother. An only brother. That was something big.

67

3. Mum and Dad

Because maybe Rob didn't care what they felt, but Stephen did.

4. moonlit domes

That wasn't to do with Rob, though. That was to do with him, his longings, that sense of strangeness, the call of the unknown.

He thought he had finished the list, but the pencil went on writing, almost without his volition, as if it had separated itself from his conscious mind. He looked down:

5. The Wart

He knew what that meant, in all its weirdness: the worst thing about Grindlesham, that should have been the best.

'Oh Christ!' he muttered.

With the rubber at the other end of the pencil, he quickly erased it.

He had expected an old man in a suit, but the consul was young, with an open shirt and his jacket flung over the back of his chair.

There was a fine view from his window over the city, down to the bright blue line of the Bosphorus, and the hills of Asia behind.

'Hello!' said the consul. 'What can I do for you?'

Stephen explained, as best he could. He knew it didn't sound too good. When he came to the bit about Jerry being arrested, he noticed the consul glanced at a file on his desk. Jerry's perhaps. He'd know more than Stephen probably.

The consul made no comment while he talked, and when Stephen had finished he sat silent for a while, looking out of the window.

'Can I see your passport?' he asked, finally.

Stephen passed it over. The consul flicked through the pages, and checked his name against a list.

'You are only fifteen?'

Stephen nodded.

'If you knew how many young people I see – boys like you mostly. And I can't help. I want to help, but what can I do? Repatriate? It's meant to be a last resort for the desperate, not an easy way to get home when you've run out of money. And the kids on drug charges... It's a horror. I have people sleeping in my flat. I lend money from my own pocket, but there's always more people coming in. But look, you're only fifteen. You shouldn't be here at all at your age. You should be back at home studying. Your parents don't appear to have reported you missing – at least you're not on my list. Not that that means anything; the system's a shambles. But if they ask me to send you back, I'll do it. Let's do it now. Here's my phone.'

He pushed an old-fashioned black telephone across the desk.

'Ring your parents. Tell them your situation. They can send money to you here to collect, in which case you can keep your passport and buy your own train ticket. If they'll do that, that's fine. Otherwise they can speak to me and I'll have you repatriated. Either way you get back home and hopefully have learnt some sense.'

He stood up.

'The telephonist will put you through. I'll leave you here to make the connection, and I'll be back in a few minutes. Good luck!'

The consul went out. For a moment Stephen wondered where he'd gone. To the toilet, perhaps. Then he wondered why he hadn't thought of phoning home before. It seemed obvious now. His parents would be furious, but they'd send money. They'd make him feel ashamed, but they'd take him in. And yet . . . And yet, now that he was about to do it, how much he didn't want to leave! Frantically, he tried to think of ways out, or at least of delaying things. Perhaps he could ask for more money than he needed, and then he could pretend he couldn't get a train ticket, and stay on a few days . . . But that would be lying. He wouldn't do that to his parents. Not that.

He picked up the phone and gave his parents' number to the telephonist.

'In England?'

'That's right. In England.'

He waited. There were whirring noises. Then another conversation between two operators that he couldn't understand. Then the sound of a telephone ringing in a house a thousand miles away. It sounded clear, but distant: his parents' phone.

He wondered what time it was there. Earlier than here, mid-morning probably. He could picture the house, only too clearly. His father wouldn't be there. He'd be at work. But his mother . . . She was probably in the garden . . . She'd be hurrying now, taking off her gardening gloves, her outdoor shoes, worried that the phone would stop ringing before she got there. She'd have that tense look on her face; she was always worried about something or other.

She was coming now. He could feel it. At any moment she would pick the phone up, and he would be hers again. He would be on his way home . . .

He took a deep breath and closed his eyes.

And something shifted in his head: he didn't have to do this. He could go back in his own time, and in his own way. He had come for Rob, but he would stay for himself. He would live cheaply and hitchhike, like everybody else. He would meet girls, he would have experiences, he would be alive.

The ringing stopped – someone was answering. His mother.

'Hello?'

With an exquisite tingle of his spine he put the phone down and stood beside it, his hand still touching the headset, breathing steadily and looking through the window down at the Bosphorus.

The consul came back in.

'Well?' he asked. 'All right?'

'Yes,' said Stephen. 'I won't bother you again.'

'Will they send you money, then?' asked the consul, with a touch of anxiety.

'Not to here,' said Stephen. 'I'll be all right, now, though. Thanks for your help.'

He would be all right. He hadn't worked out all the

details yet, but he would be. He still had twenty pounds. To half the people in this city, it was a fortune.

He took a bus back. It was surprisingly easy. He just said, 'Blue Mosque!' and everybody helped him. The bus dropped him by the mosque, and he stood on the pavement for a few moments, watching the people in the gardens and the huge shape of the mosque behind them.

He was his own master, dependent on no one, not even Jerry, freer than he had ever been in his life.

He decided to go inside.

There was a row of beggars at the entrance: the blind, the lame, the insane – human beings like him, but with far less than he had. He gave a little money to each of them, and then he went up a flight of stairs to a courtyard, the cluster of domes and minarets looming above him.

He took off his shoes and stepped inside.

He was enveloped in blue light, coming through stained glass windows high up in the domes, and reflected off thousands of blue tiles covered in swirling arabesques. The floor was covered in rich carpets. It was quiet except for the hum of prayers from a few of the faithful, bowing towards Mecca.

He sat down beside a pillar and crossed his legs. There were other foreigners there too, sitting quietly, awed by the space and quietness, as well as a camera-clad throng that came in, looked, and passed on. He sat for a long while. He would have liked to pray, but he didn't know how. Nobody minded how long he sat there anyway. An old man with a red beard nodded at him gravely, as if to say welcome. There was an atmosphere here that he had not felt when he went with his parents to church, or in the school chapel, a presence that he could not explain. A vastness into which his small consciousness might momentarily merge.

Back at the Oteli Gulhane, the first thing he did was to agree the exchange of his suitcase for a second-hand rucksack and a thin sleeping bag, supplied by the manager. The rucksack was smaller than his suitcase, but that was no bad thing. If he was going to hitchhike back to England, then the lighter his luggage the better.

Then he booked a space on the matted floor of the Tent, for three lire.

'Valuables you can leave with me,' said the manager as he led him up the narrow stairs to the rooftop. 'Otherwise it is quite safe. Very nice. Friendly actually.'

'Are there police raids?' asked Stephen.

'Oh yes, police are coming regularly. But first they tell me, and I tell you, so no problem. Only if someone is dealing too much hash, better they go another hotel. That will not be your problem, I think.'

The Tent was just as Mary had described it. He had hoped to see her there, but it was fairly empty. A few bodies lay in sleeping bags. A little group at one end were sharing a joint. A girl lay reading. There was a smell of hash and old socks.

Stephen found a space, rolled out his new sleeping bag

and put the rucksack and suitcase next to each other.

'I'll bring down the suitcase as soon as I've re-packed,' he said.

'No hurry. Take your time,' said the manager, and left him to it.

Stephen sat down and looked around him. There was no privacy at all, but it was okay, friendly in a way, a big, primitive dormitory. There was a pot-bellied stove at one end – it was warm enough now from the sunshine, but it would get cold at night with the corrugated iron roof. All the walls were painted or crayoned in swirling designs featuring snow-capped mountains and mushrooms and wizards and beautiful, mysterious women – opium dreams, perhaps.

He opened his suitcase.

It had been packed for a different journey, and most of the contents were useless to him now. He picked out his patent leather shoes, wondering what to do with them; he'd never wear them here, though he'd need them when he was back at school. But he didn't want to even think about that.

He pulled out his dirty underwear, and made a smelly heap beside the rucksack. He'd have to get it washed, somehow. Mary had said the hotel had a laundry service; he hoped it wouldn't be too expensive.

He kept smelling hashish. He supposed it came from the group in the corner, but it seemed to have attached itself to the suitcase.

Underneath the clothes were his writing pad and some

books that he'd packed expecting lots of long boring evenings, and forgotten about: *After Many a Summer* by Aldous Huxley. Rob had been into Huxley, he remembered. *The Catcher in The Rye* by J.D. Salinger. The Wart had recommended that. *The Carpet Baggers* by Harold Robbins. Fat and trashy. He might enjoy them now. He could lie on his mattress and read all day, and then he could sell them or swap them. It would be better than going straight home.

Into *The Catcher in the Rye* he had slipped a photo. He took it out. It was of his father and mother, standing in front of their house – his mother small, slightly stooped, his father militarily straight, with his white hair combed over his bald patch. They were smiling for the camera, but they were standing apart, not touching.

Stephen looked at the picture, with a mixture of emotions. He felt love, certainly. He missed them in a way. But more powerfully, he felt sorry for them, their oldness, the grey emptiness of their lives. Rob had hurt them terribly, by running away and then disappearing. Stephen would never do that to them. He promised himself he would never do that to them.

As soon as he went out again, he would go to the post office and send them a telegram. Tell them he'd be home soon.

The smell of hashish seemed to be growing stronger.

There was a side pocket on his suitcase that he never used, but now that the suitcase was almost empty, he realised there was something inside it. Another book, perhaps. Funny, because he didn't remember packing it. For a moment he hoped that it might be a big bar of chocolate that his mother had slipped in without telling him, as a treat. He really fancied some chocolate.

But his mother didn't do things like that.

He unzipped the pocket and pulled out a rectangular package.

Suddenly he was aware of every little sound in the room. He looked furtively around, but no one was paying him any attention. He slipped the package out of his suitcase, so that he could see it properly, but he already knew what it was. And he knew now only too well how dangerous it was.

It was a block of hashish. A large block.

He quickly slid it into his rucksack, and sat with his heart pumping, frozen like a rabbit.

Part 2:
Journey to the East

I've seen archipelagos of stars! and islands
Whose delirious skies lie open to the wanderer.
Arthur Rimbaud: *The Drunken Boat*

Chapter 8

Stephen sat immobile on his sleeping bag for a long time. He knew how the hash had got in his suitcase. There was only one possibility. Jerry must have put it there when he sent Stephen out to get the nuts.

But that didn't matter now. Jerry was in prison, and Stephen had the hash. It must be worth money – a lot probably. But it was also dangerous. If he sold it, he was a drug dealer. If he kept it, the police might arrest him. He could try throwing it away, take it and chuck it in the Bosphorus... or he could give it away... but who to?

He had no idea what he should do. Who could he trust? He had never felt so alone.

He sat looking at his suitcase and his useless clothes. The group at the end of the room finished their joint, and lay back on their mattresses, talking quietly in German, with occasional bursts of laughter.

'Hey, man, I know you, right!'

Someone was standing behind him. Stephen started, and looked round. It was Martin, the long-haired boy who had been caught by the customs.

Stephen was taken aback for a moment. He hadn't expected to see Martin. He thought he was in prison, like Jerry.

'Oh, yes, hello,' he said.

'Hey, man, good you get here!' said Martin.

'Are you okay? I mean, at the customs, did they let you go, then?'

'The customs? Oh yeah. That man's a bastard, but he let me go, he even let me keep my hash. Because he only want one thing. I give it him, he's happy.'

'What thing's that?' asked Stephen, puzzled.

Martin looked down at him, and smiled. It wasn't a very attractive smile. He had a line of black between his front teeth, and a sore on his lower lip.

'What you think a guy like him want? You're pretty enough, you'll find out. You want to buy some hash? I got real good quality...'

'No thanks,' said Stephen.

Martin shrugged and ambled off to join the group of smokers in the corner.

Stephen sat on his sleeping bag, and absent-mindedly carried on sorting through his things, lining up his ties and his suit and his shoes and wondering what to do with them. There certainly wouldn't be room for them in the rucksack. He thought about the consul, wishing he had taken his advice. More than anything, he just wanted to go home, the quickest way possible.

Morosely, he put his ties on top of his shoes, and stuffed his soiled underwear into the rucksack.

It was evening and the Tent was filling up. People came in and sat in small groups, chatting and smoking. Someone started playing a guitar. Stephen carried on sitting, but after a while he propped his rucksack against the wall, and lay back against it. He felt a little calmer. After all, it wasn't the end of the world.

How much was the hash worth? He had no idea. But if he sold it, he might be able to afford a train ticket.

The idea of hitchhiking those long empty roads that he had travelled so easily with the green bus had lost its attraction. He wanted to be back in his own bed, with his mother nagging him and the April sunshine playing on the daffodils.

If he could sell the hash . . . if he could get fifty dollars for it, he'd have enough for a train ticket. It might be worth fifty dollars. Perhaps he should ask Martin.

Or perhaps not. If he couldn't trust Jerry, how could he trust Martin?

How could he trust anybody?

A wave of shame and fear came over him. He'd trusted Jerry – he'd seemed like such a nice guy. But Jerry had just been using him all along, first to guard the van, so that he could make love to Astrid in hotel bedrooms, and then to hide his hash . . . It was only luck that Stephen wasn't in jail with Jerry now.

He'd been a fool. A total idiot.

You couldn't trust anybody. He knew that now.

He sensed someone approaching, and looked up and saw Mary.

'Hello again. So here you are!' she said. 'Are you leaving on the train tonight, then?'

'I don't think so,' said Stephen.

She looked at him closely.

'You don't look too good. Has something happened? Are you all right?'

For a moment he wanted to take her into his confidence, but he stopped himself. He wouldn't make that mistake again.

'I'm fine,' he said, forcing a smile. 'It's just that this rucksack I got is too small to fit my things in.'

'I'll help you pack it. I'm really good at that,' she said.

'No! No!' he stopped her. 'I . . . I'd rather not.'

'Please yourself! Do you fancy coming out for a meal, then?'

'No, I . . .'

Stephen looked around. He suddenly realised how hungry he was, and in one way he would have loved to go out with Mary to eat. But he was scared to leave the hash in his rucksack, and he was worried about Mary too. She saw through him too easily. He'd never be able to keep it secret.

'Worried about leaving your things here, are you?' she asked. 'It's safe enough actually. We leave our stuff here, no problem, but then we don't have anything worth stealing. But if you're worried, just pack it all up and leave it with the manager. He'll put it in his lock-up. Leave your sleeping bag though, to keep your place. Brian!'

One of the sleeping bags opposite stirred and a tousle-headed man sat up and looked over.

'You woken up yet?'

'I was reading,' said Brian.

'Come on, we're going to eat.'

82

'Oh yeah,' said Brian. 'Is it that time already? Let's have a joint first.'

'All right, but get a bit of a move on,' said Mary. She went over to the mattress next to Brian, and sat down leaning against the wall and stretching out her legs.

'By the way, this is Brian, who I came here with. Brian, this is Stephen.'

'Hi!' said Brian, putting his cigarette lighter to a small piece of hash and watching the smoke curl up.

'Come over here and sit with us,' said Mary. 'Your bag won't disappear while you're looking at it. Do you smoke dope, by the way?'

'Not really,' said Stephen.

He stood up awkwardly and came and sat between Mary and Brian.

'Better not,' said Mary. 'Look at Brian. He can't hardly move any more, he's so stoned all the time. It doesn't affect me though. I just get a bit giggly.'

'Great shit though, this,' said Brian. 'Afghani. Number One Mindfuck! Blows your head away.'

He finished rolling his joint, lit it and inhaled deeply, then let out a great cloud of smoke and doubled up coughing.

Mary flashed a grin at Stephen. Brian was holding out the joint. She reached over and took it and puffed at it. She wasn't really inhaling, Stephen thought. The pungent smoke drifted past his nostrils, so that he couldn't help breathing it in.

Suddenly he was hit by a wave of paranoia. Why had they got him here? What did they want from him?

He stood up.

'I'll take my things down to the manager, and go out for a bit,' he said.

'Don't you want to come out and eat with us?' Mary smiled at him.

'No thanks,' said Stephen, looking away.

'Please yourself,' said Mary, with a shrug.

Stephen wrapped his shoes in his suit and stuffed everything else into the rucksack. It was surprising how much he could fit in, now he tried. He could feel Mary and Brian watching him, but he didn't look round, just picked up the bags and hurried to the door.

'See you later, man. Take care,' Brian called after him, but Stephen didn't turn round.

He felt better outside. It was growing dark and the clamour of the city was wrapped in mysterious light.

As he came out into the gardens by the Blue Mosque, there was a crackle of loudspeakers, and then the now familiar sound of the muezzin:

Allahu Akbar Allahu Akbar Allahu Akbar

'God is great!' said a voice behind him.

'What?'

'God is great. That's what it means. God is Great. There is no God but God, and Allah is his prophet. Far out, huh?'

Stephen turned to see Reuben, Jerry's friend from the Pudding Shop.

'Hey, kid, good to see you. Where's Jerry?'

84

'Jerry's been arrested,' said Stephen, before he could stop himself.

Reuben's face fell.

'Jerry, man? You're not serious? Arrested? Not for dope, man? Don't say it's for dope!'

It was too late to hide anything now.

'Yes,' said Stephen. 'Last night. The police came to the hotel.'

'Hey, we got to talk about this,' said Reuben, leading him to the Pudding Shop.

Stephen didn't really want another pudding. He wanted a proper meal, with brown beans and mutton, and thick gravy to slop his bread into. But he had one anyway; it was better than nothing.

'That's terrible, man.' Reuben shook his head. 'Those cops are real bastards. They searched his room, right?'

Stephen nodded.

'Did they find a lot of dope?'

'I don't know,' said Stephen, truthfully.

'What about you? Did they search your room too?'

'No,' said Stephen. Reuben kept looking at him, expecting him to say more, so he added:

'Well, they just looked in, but they didn't really search my bag or anything.'

Reuben shook his head again.

'It's bad, man. Hope they didn't find too much on Jerry. Because I heard he just scored a couple of K. Did he tell you anything about that?'

Reuben was looking at Stephen. His eyes were big and brown. Like deep pools. Powerful, but kind, Stephen thought.

'I'd like to help Jerry, man,' said Reuben softly. 'I'd like to help you too. You're on your own here now. Your money's running out, I'll bet. You could do with some friends, kid.'

Reuben leant back and lit a cigarette.

'Knowing Jerry, I'll bet he'd have hidden that hash pretty well, before the cops came. Huh?'

'Yes...' Stephen started. Then he stopped. Reuben pulled at his cigarette, and watched him patiently. Stephen wanted to trust him. He wanted to tell him about the hash in his suitcase. He wanted to give this problem to someone else.

'You can trust me,' said Reuben, smiling kindly. 'I'm a friend.'

But whose friend? Jerry's? Suddenly Stephen was on his guard again.

'Yes,' he said abruptly. 'I'm sure he would have hidden it, but he didn't tell me. I don't even smoke the stuff. I'm going to go and get myself a meal now.'

He stood up, and walked to the counter to pay.

Reuben came behind him.

'I mean it, man. If you need any help here, I'm your guy. I'll go check out what's happening with Jerry in the morning. Say, where're you staying now?'

Stephen stopped and turned to him.

'What makes you think I've moved?'

'Hey,' said Reuben. 'Don't get funny with me, man. I'm trying to help you.'

'Thanks,' said Stephen. Suddenly he felt ashamed. Why was he so suspicious of everyone? 'If you do hear anything about Jerry, I'd like to know…'

They were in the street again.

'Don't worry,' said Reuben. 'I'll be seeing you!'

He winked, and strolled off into the night.

'Have you eaten then, already?'

Stephen started. It was Mary. She'd been standing there by the doorway with her scarf over her head, and he hadn't seen her.

'No,' he said. 'Just a pudding. I'm sick of puddings.'

'Come on then,' said Mary.

'Where's Brian?' asked Stephen.

'I couldn't move him at all, and I got fed up with waiting. I'm glad I found you. I don't like eating alone. Come on, there's a great little restaurant round the corner.'

'That guy you were talking to, he gives me the creeps,' said Mary.

'Reuben?'

'That's his name, is it?' said Mary. 'He's always hanging about the Pudding Shop, making out he's matey-matey with everyone. I've heard he's a police informer, or maybe a CIA agent.'

'What? Who said that?'

'Brian. he knows about things like that. What's the guy

hanging about you for, though? You don't look like you've got much to inform about, if you don't mind my saying so. Oh!'

She stopped, with a piece of bread half way to her mouth and stared at Stephen.

'It's your friend, isn't it? The one who was busted. Oh, I'm sorry. I'm only poking my nose where it's not wanted as usual. Forget I asked. This is a great stew, isn't it?'

Stephen felt himself shaking. He had almost told Reuben about the hash. And Reuben seemed to suspect anyway that he had it – how did he know that? As soon as he got back to the hotel, Stephen decided, he would wrap the hash in his vest and throw it in the Bosphorus. That was the only safe thing.

Thank God he hadn't told Reuben where he was staying.

He looked across at Mary. She was eating, absorbed in the food, but she felt his gaze, and looked up and grinned at him, almost shyly.

He had to trust someone. He couldn't carry this alone. And better Mary than Reuben, any day.

'Can you keep a secret?' he said.

'What are you going to do with the hash then?' asked Mary as they walked back to the hotel.

'I think I'll throw it away,' said Stephen. 'I'm not a drug dealer, and I don't want to be. It's too dangerous.'

Mary stopped in her tracks.

'Throw it away? You can't do that.'

'What if Reuben finds out where I'm staying and tells the police?'

'He doesn't know anything. You didn't tell him anything. But you're right, you should get rid of it, but not throw it away. It's worth good money.'

'I don't know how to sell it. I wouldn't know how to begin.'

'Just give it to Brian. He's a complete dope-head, but he's honest, and he's got the contacts. He'll get you a fair price. That's what you'd like, isn't it? Another fifty dollars, so you can pay for your train ticket home, and forget about your brother. Isn't that right?'

'Yes, I suppose so.'

They walked on.

'What I don't get is, why do you want to go home anyway?' asked Mary. 'It doesn't sound like much of a fun place to me.'

'I have to go back to school,' said Stephen.

Mary almost snorted.

'School? School? Oh, do you like school then?'

She turned to him, her eyes glittering with mockery.

'No, of course not. But I'm doing my O-levels this summer...' He trailed off.

'O-levels!' said Mary scornfully. 'Really? Is that all?'

'No,' said Stephen. 'There's my mother. She was so devastated when Rob went away. I just remember how she looked – still looks quite often. She was different before that, I'm sure she was. I can't do that to her.'

'You already have,' said Mary.

They walked on silently for a while.

'I'll tell you what,' said Mary suddenly. 'I'll tell you this for free, and then I won't say another word about it. I don't think you should just go straight back home with your tail between your legs. I think you should finish what you came for. I think you should find your brother, now you've found out where he is. If you don't, you'll spend the rest of your life regretting it.'

'But Rob's in Afghanistan. It's miles away.'

'It's not so far. Just a few days of bus-rides. And the further East you go the cheaper it gets. You can live for a year in Afghanistan on fifty dollars! That's what I've heard. That's where I'm going anyway. I'm giving up on Brian. He'll never move. So I'll go on my own. Unless you want to come with me.'

They stepped out of a side street, and there was the Blue Mosque. They both looked up at the illuminated domes.

'I love the road,' said Mary. 'I love the feeling that you can just go on and on, and never go back. It's exciting, isn't it? To cross the Bosphorus into Asia, and on over the mountains and through the desert: there'll be camels and eagles and wild tribes of nomads, and rose gardens and holy men and oases. And then beyond that there's India, and ancient cities, and beaches with palm trees, and elephants...and then there's Katmandhu...and Burma...and Japan...Such a big world out there. All waiting for us to explore it. And it's real. Not just something in a book. Real. I can't wait.'

90

She turned to Stephen.

'Come with me,' she said. 'Go on, come with me!'

'I don't know,' said Stephen.

It had been a long day, Stephen reflected as he lay in his sleeping bag in the Tent. There was a hum of talk and soft laughter from a group clustered around the pot-bellied stove, now lit and mingling wood-smoke with the smell of hashish. The 40-watt bulb had been switched off, and candlelight flickered on the garish murals. A long day. A long journey. A big world.

One thing he had forgotten to do – he had forgotten to send his parents a telegram.

He would do it first thing in the morning.

And he would send his clothes to a laundry.

And he would take a bath. There were Turkish baths here, called hamams. Mary had told him.

How did she always know about everything?

Because she experienced the world, rather than learning about it in books, like he'd done. School was a waste of time really.

Perhaps it wasn't so hard to go to Afghanistan, find Rob. If Rob existed.

Was Rob a dream?

He would decide tomorrow. He would decide in the morning…

Chapter 9

'Whatever you do, don't take the train!'

That had been the advice of a guy in the Pudding Shop, accompanied by garish stories of rapes and slit throats. But Mary and Stephen did take the train, third class: three days through the middle of Turkey, from Ankara to Erzurum. It was simply the cheapest way. And though people stared, no one molested them.

It was slow, though, chugging laboriously up mountain range after mountain range, each wilder than the last.

There was time to think – too much, perhaps – time to remember, in the jolting, crowded railway carriage moving inexorably into the unknown. And the further Stephen travelled, the more urgently the past – his other world – kept coming back to him.

Stephen had had his fifteenth birthday in the summer holidays – his first birthday without Rob – and though his parents tried their best, it was pretty dull. His mother gave him a suitcase and his father gave him a fountain pen, and his aunt and uncle and his cousin Harriet came over, but none of them could forget about Rob, ever-present in his absence.

The whole summer was dismal. They didn't attempt a holiday. For the first time in his life, Stephen was glad when September came and he had a haircut and put on his suit and his father drove him back to

Grindlesham, his boarding school.

Rob had been chucked out before he even went there, but people still talked about him – Mad Dog Wiston, who won both the Pilkington Essay Prize and the Heatherington Trench award for Latin Hexameters when he was fifteen, who hit a six through the pavilion window, who shot at prefects with an air rifle, and who one night drove a herd of cows from a neighbouring field into the toilet block, and never got caught.

Stephen wondered why his parents had sent him to the same school, but the answer was simple – they blamed Rob, not the school.

Anyway, although Stephen looked like Rob, he wasn't a bit like him otherwise, and couldn't have been if he'd wanted to be. He never did anything wrong, and he never won a prize.

Most of the teachers quickly saw this, breathed a sigh of relief, and ignored him. Lessons were dull, and games were something he just didn't seem to understand.

'The trouble with you, Wiston, is that you lack competitive spirit,' said Mr Husting, his housemaster. 'Look at you, big strong boy! You've got an eye for a ball too. You could be in the school cricket team if you pulled a finger out.'

'It's just, I don't see the point, Sir. I mean, if one side wins the other side loses.'

'That's exactly what I mean. It's your attitude that's the problem. Where's your drive, boy? You'll never get anywhere in life with an attitude like that.'

93

Stephen felt puzzled and a little hurt. He knew that his attitude to sport was a real deficiency, because it cut him off from the others. He had tried. For a while he supported a football team, because that was what the other boys did, but he just couldn't work up any enthusiasm. He couldn't see what was so wonderful about winning a match if you weren't even playing, and besides he always felt sorry for the losers. Yet he didn't want to be different, and he would have liked to talk about this with Mr Husting, but Mr Husting clearly only felt scorn.

Although Stephen wasn't unpopular, he had little in common with most of the other boys. He wasn't much interested in pop music, or the grubby copies of *Titbits* that circulated in the dormitory. He spotted the bullies quickly and avoided them – he was too strong and good-looking to be a victim. He made friends with other outsiders, a tall and unnaturally thin boy named Strichton, but always called Strychnine, who spent every spare minute in the art room making giant sculptures out of yoghurt pots and fairy lights; and an overweight boy called Potter, who knew everything there was to know about fossils.

By the start of his second year, he was neither happy nor unhappy. Life was dull at home and it was dull at school. He didn't expect anything different. It was as if he was half asleep, a characteristic his teachers sometimes noted in their reports. 'Could do with a bit less dreaming and a bit more application to the subject,' was a typical comment. At home he often went to the cinema with his one friend, Pete, but at school there was no access to cinema or television, so he read. He read slowly, often not taking much in, or re-reading the same paragraph over and over again. And when no one was bothering him, he would let the book drop and shut his eyes, and let long fantasies unroll on the inside of his eyelids, fantasies that were far more vivid than his so-called reality. He had always done this, since he could remember, but now the fantasies had taken new twists. Twists that involved girls.

These were not the pneumatic images from *Titbits*, but more like real girls who wore clothes and had breath that smelled of new dug earth or stewed apricots, and talked to him, and lay under the stars, and kissed him gently and then not so gently... until one day a huge spurt of semen erupted all over his trousers and he felt as though the earth was caving in around him and the blood pounded in his head, and left him gasping, suddenly aware of two things – that this was what all those books were about, this was sex – or was it just masturbation? And that the girl who a moment before had been caressing him under the trees in a bluebell wood, had disintegrated back into the reality of his squalid bed in his squalid cubicle in his squalid boarding school.

Outside of his fantasies, Stephen was bored and lonely. But he accepted it, because this was the only state he could remember.

Then came the Wart.

Mr Wortle was not quite like the other teachers. He was gentle, and he was observant, and he was funny. He mostly taught A-level English and History, but he took some lower classes as well, to see what talent might be developing among the younger boys. He kept discipline effortlessly, without raising his voice. For the first time, Stephen found himself enjoying his lessons. They revived memories of Rob, sitting on the end of his bed and reading from Yeats, or Blake, or Shelley, or Dylan Thomas.

'Don't worry what it means. Just listen and let it go inside you,' Rob had said, and Mr Wortle said something similar. And it was true. He opened himself to the poems and the phrases stuck: *'Rage, rage against the dying of the light!' 'To see a world in a grain of sand.' 'Look on my works ye mighty and despair.'*

They seemed to be messages from inner worlds like his own. Certainly they had nothing to do with the drab world he saw around him. His mother cried sometimes, but she didn't rage, there was no passion or despair, just sullen misery like a wet November day.

Mr Wortle taught him Shakespeare. At first Stephen found it hard to understand, but as Mr Wortle brought the words to life in the classroom, he realised it was easy – a few obscure words and turns of speech to be understood and remembered, and he had the keys to unlock the Elizabethan language. They were doing *A Midsummer Night's Dream*, and Stephen found there dreams and visions stranger than anything his own mind had ever conjured. And just as erotic. The drugged lovers, lusting after the wrong person; the fairy caressing the idiot with the ass's head . . . strange, heightened worlds – unless it was the school that was strange, and his dull home and the dull streets and his parents' tedious friends. What would he have given to shift his reality, to be Puck, or Lysander, or even Bottom, and to stay in that world forever?

'Remarkable effort!' said Mr Wortle, handing back an essay towards the end of term. 'Remarkable! I have great hopes of you, Wiston. You have real sensibility. Tell me, do you write poetry?'

Stephen blushed. 'Sometimes, Sir,' he mumbled, not wanting the other boys to hear.

'I thought as much. Anyway, well done.'

He came top in English. It was the first time he had ever been top in anything. His parents were delighted.

'I told you the school would come up trumps in the end,' said his father. 'That Mr Wortle will certainly bring him on.'

During the last summer term Mr Wortle had started his Junior Poetry Group. They met in Mr Wortle's flat, or outside in the grounds in fine weather, to read and discuss poetry. Stephen was the first boy that Mr Wortle asked, and in a way he felt that the whole group was because of him. He didn't say so, but he felt flattered. Mr Wortle was the first adult who had ever noticed him, ever found him special, ever picked out his uniqueness from the shadow of his brilliant older brother.

'Yes, your brother,' said Mr Wortle one day. They were walking back to the college after a meeting under the Great Oak, and the others had run ahead. 'Robert, I believe. A talented boy, indeed. Do you hear from him at all?'

'No,' admitted Stephen. 'We haven't heard for ages. We don't know where he is or anything. My mother called the police. She thinks he's dead. But they can't do anything.'

Mr Wortle stopped, and looked at Stephen closely. He had clear green eyes in an otherwise uneventful face.

'Do *you* think he's dead?' he asked gently.

'Not really,' said Stephen.

'I'm sure he isn't,' said Mr Wortle. 'My impression of your brother was that he would go his own way in life, and that he was well able to take care of himself. More like you than one might imagine, perhaps. Still, it must be a great sadness for you. I'm sure you miss him terribly.'

They walked on silently. Stephen struggled to hold back his tears. He didn't understand why Mr Wortle's words of sympathy made him so emotional, and he didn't want anyone to see.

He did miss Rob. That was the point. He did miss him terribly. And yet, beside his mother's misery, his own counted for nothing. His father had patted him on the shoulder after the policeman had called, and then said:

'We have to look after your mother. Make sure that she is all right, that's the main thing.'

Mr Wortle's simple words of sympathy released his grief. Back in his cubicle, he hugged his pillow and wept freely for the first time.

The Junior Poetry Group flourished. It was a fine summer, and they met mainly under the Great Oak, a tree at the edge of the cricket field with a vast trunk and shrunken canopy, that was recorded in the Domesday Book. Stephen hadn't thought that anyone else in the school cared about poetry, or would admit it if they did, but there were about ten members, including Strychnine.

'I didn't know you were interested in poetry, Strych,' said Stephen, after the first time he came.

Strychnine jigged about a bit in a way he had.

'It depends what you mean by poetry,' he said.

That summer, all over Europe and America, youth was stirring, with new music, new fashions, new rhythms, new ways of thought, but not much of it reached Grindlesham. None of them, not even Mr Wortle, knew about Allen Ginsberg's visit to Europe, and the huge event planned to take place in the Albert Hall that summer, that would transform the image of poetry. The school remained an unchanged world of short-haired boys in jackets and ties; music meant Mozart and Beethoven, novels were by Dickens and Hardy, and most poets were long dead.

Mr Wortle read the poetry group 'The Hollow Men' by T.S. Eliot. It was a vivid image: men like scarecrows, hollow, stuffed, with heads filled with straw.

'It was after the first world war,' he commented. 'That's how it felt. It was the same after the second world war, though perhaps less so. In an odd way, wars give people purpose, you take that away and you feel only half alive.'

It made Stephen think of his father. Was he a hollow man? Was he a stuffed man, headpiece filled with straw?

He had hardly seen his father for the first eight years of his life, because he had been away in the army, stationed at places like Aden, that were thought – by his mother at least – to be too dangerous to bring up children. His father was a picture on the mantelpiece, a promised excitement at Christmas that did not long outlive the initial thrill of a present. Rob nailed him with crude humour. 'The man who wasn't there', he called him, after the nonsense rhyme:

> *As I was going up the stair*
> *I met a man who wasn't there.*
> *He wasn't there again today –*
> *Oh, how I wish he'd go away.*

Stephen didn't wish that his father would go away, though. He liked him. He wasn't close, because you couldn't be, but he liked his presence, liked sitting with him in the study. When he was younger he used to ask him questions.

'What did you do in the war, Dad?' he asked once.

For a moment, a look of panic crossed his father's usually calm face.

'I don't think you'd want to know,' he said, taking out his pipe.

Stephen didn't ask again.

Strychnine brought a book into the poetry group.

'My uncle sent me this from New York. My uncle's a bit weird,' he added apologetically. He was nervous about showing it to a teacher, but Mr Wortle took the slim volume and read the first lines out loud.

'I saw the best minds of my generation destroyed by madness, starving hysterical naked,'

A couple of boys tittered at the word naked. Mr Wortle ignored them.

'dragging themselves through the negro streets at dawn looking for an angry fix . . .'

He stopped abruptly.

'Could I borrow it?' he asked Strychnine. 'I'd like to read it at my leisure.'

He returned it the next week without comment. Stephen and Strych puzzled over the poem together but aside from a few references to drugs and some dirty words they couldn't puzzle out much meaning.

Poetry was often like that, Stephen thought. You didn't know what it meant, but it stayed with you all the same. Hollow men. Stuffed men.

'Poetry isn't about giving information, it's about experience. That's why young men are often so much better at it than old men. Whatever the poets say, they're not lying, and they're not giving it second-hand. They write what they have lived, or it's bogus.'

So said Mr Wortle. They were sitting under the Great Oak on a still June evening. There was a cricket match in progress, and the other boys had wandered over to watch it, but Stephen lingered, enjoying the aftertaste of the poems they'd read together.

With a shy smile, as if he didn't mean it, Mr Wortle put his hand on Stephen's knee.

'Hey look!' said Mary. 'There's eagles!'

She had put her hand on his knee to get his attention. He started in surprise and jerked his knee, and she moved it at once and pointed out of the train window.

'Look!'

They were going up a ravine, so slowly it seemed to Stephen he could have got out and walked alongside the train. When he craned forward, he could see the crags above them, and, yes, eagles circling.

'They say there's wolves here, too,' said Mary. Stephen stared at the rocks and small shrubs, half expecting to see a wolf. Instead he saw clusters of bright yellow flowers, and what looked like tiny red tulips poking up among the grasses.

Opposite them sat an old peasant couple, who had stared at them solidly without speaking for the last sixteen hours. Stephen had tried smiling at them, but had no response.

'It's better if they don't smile,' said Mary. 'I think smiling means something different here. All the people trying to rip you off or sell you something smile all the time, but I think the ones who don't smile are all right.'

Like the man in the restaurant in Ankara. After they had eaten, and tried to pay, the waiter had simply said, 'It's paid for!' and when they asked further, gestured to a man with a red beard at the other end of the restaurant, who nodded at them gravely.

'Why?' asked Stephen. 'Why should he pay for us?'

'You are guests of our country,' said the waiter, as if it was obvious.

Nonetheless, it was disconcerting to be stared at so continuously, like a freak show.

'Where were you, anyway?' asked Mary.

'What do you mean?'

'In your thoughts. You were miles away.'

'I was thinking about my school,' Stephen admitted.

'I'm sure that was a bundle of fun.'

'I don't know,' said Stephen. 'It's a long way from here, isn't it?'

'You can say that again!'

'What was your school like?'

'Mine? Terrible. I couldn't get out of there fast enough. It was the other kids mostly, not the teachers. Some of the teachers were all right. I had a great Geography teacher... But I was always going to get away, anyway. It was all I thought about, leaving home and seeing what the rest of the world was like. I didn't want to hear about it, I wanted to see it.'

There was a hoot and a blast of steam from in front, and the train picked up some speed. They looked out of the window. The gorge had opened up, and they had reached a watershed – a wide valley with green meadows still patched with snow, and a pretty village. A boy was running after some goats that had been frightened by the train. In front the land fell away, and in the distance were vistas of endless further mountains.

Mary looked round at Stephen. Her eyes were blood-shot from travelling, but they shone all the same. She was smiling excitedly.

'Isn't it great? Isn't it bloody fantastic to be here?'

Chapter 10

It was a hard and dangerous journey, and seemed to take forever.

They rested for a day in Erzurum, in Eastern Turkey, where grizzled men with rifles sold wolf skins, and women in full veils wove through the bazaar like black ghosts. The winter ice had not yet melted from the streets and the nights were terribly cold.

They seemed to be the only foreigners in the town.

'You know what?' said Stephen. 'I never sent a telegram to my parents. I meant to do that before we left Istanbul.'

They were sitting in a café by the bus stand, sipping black tea and watching the dilapidated buses unloading.

'There's got to be a post office here somewhere,' said Mary. 'I mean, we're not on the moon or anything, are we? Let's do it now.'

There was a post office, though it took them an hour to find it, and when they did, it was closed. It was a public holiday.

Then they met a group of students, and went and drank coffee with them.

They left for the Iranian border at five o'clock the next morning, along with a goat and several chickens, in an ancient bus that never looked as if it would get very far. It was freezing hard. The tarmac came to a sudden end a few miles out of town, and after that they bumped along a gravel road for a few hours, stopping frequently to let people on and off. The bus juddered and stuttered, and then finally broke down on the outskirts of a village. The driver shouted something, and everybody got out, Stephen and Mary with them.

They stood on the roadside. The driver opened the bonnet, and a cloud of steam came out. The driver shrugged. It didn't look hopeful.

All they could do was wait. The sun had risen, and had already taken the iciness out of the air. A group of children gathered round them, staring. Mary was edgy, and adjusted her scarf so that it covered her mouth.

'Whatever you do, don't touch me,' she muttered to Stephen. 'Men and women just don't do that here, and when they see Westerners doing it, they think we're immoral. And try not to look back at them when they stare at us, either. We don't want any trouble.'

But Stephen couldn't help looking at the ring of faces. They weren't hostile, he thought. Just curious, as if they were watching monkeys in a zoo. And after a while, their curiosity faded, and they lost interest.

For a long time, nothing much happened. The driver had disappeared, and most of the passengers squatted beside the road, smoking, chatting, or staring into the distance. Others had wandered off in the direction of the village. The goat was tethered by a patch of thorns, and the chickens sat in the dust, their legs tied together to prevent escape.

Occasionally a bus passed and some of the men would run into the road shouting to it to stop, with no result except a hooting of the horn and a cloud of dust.

Stephen began to worry that they would be there forever.

'What's happening?' he asked Mary. 'Surely they can't leave us here?'

Mary was squatting down by the roadside like the other women. She grinned up at him mischievously.

'Calm down, Stephen. Where would you rather be, anyway? At school?'

At that moment an empty, open truck pulled up beside them. Everybody started shouting, and then clambered up into the back, along with the goat and the chickens.

As they set off, the driver's assistant – a boy of about twelve – jumped up over the side and went round collecting money.

'Will you pay for both of us?' said Mary. 'It'll look better. Don't worry, I'll pay you back.'

Stephen looked in his pocket for coins, but he could only find a note. It was too much, he knew. Probably much too much, and he was sure the boy wouldn't give him any change. The boy hardly looked at the note, but he stared at Stephen with a grin and slightly glazed eyes, as if struggling to remember something, then said, 'Good morning!'

'Good morning to you,' Stephen replied. The boy turned to everyone with a look of delight, and said something in Turkish that made them all laugh. Then, flushed with his success, he turned back to Stephen and announced:

'Manchester United! Bobby Charlton!'

Stephen nodded, and grinned back.

'Very good!' he replied, but the boy had exhausted his vocabulary. He counted out the change quickly and precisely, then without warning jumped over the side of the truck, opening the door of the cab and slipping inside without it slowing down, James Bond-style.

Nobody had taken any notice of Mary. There were so many stories of Western women being raped and molested in these wild lands, but Mary was never touched. Stephen watched her, sitting on the floor of the truck next to the Turkish women, her scarf tight around her, and her face hardly visible. She looked like one of them. And they warmed to her too, he could see that. As he watched, one of the women started showing Mary her baby.

She was amazing, Stephen thought, the way she read every situation as it came, the way she became invisible when she needed to, the way she never complained about hard seats or bed-bugs or diarrhoea. He couldn't have wanted a better travelling companion... And yet...

And yet she wasn't Astrid.

Not that she wasn't attractive. She had a sweet face and a slim, strong body. But she was simply too real for him. And as Astrid faded into the past, the memory of her, her long fingers and the way she flicked back her hair, grew only more beguiling. That time in Greece... What if Jerry hadn't reappeared?

The wind was cold, but the sun was burning his head. He took out a floppy hat that he'd picked up in Istanbul. Mary didn't like it, because it looked wrong and attracted attention, but he didn't care. He pulled it on tight and stood behind the cab, holding onto the frame for balance and looking out at the arid, snow-flecked plateau.

They had been going steadily uphill for a couple of hours, but now they came to the top of the pass, and Mount Ararat swung into view, huge and white, clouds forming around its summit.

This mountain was nothing like the Alps. It stood alone on a desolate plateau, immense and solid. Yet at the same time it was unearthly, dreamlike, not of this world and not of this time. Biblical, perhaps...

Involuntarily, he thought of Thierry and Charleville. He should be there now. What day was it? He always had to count.

The truck bounced noisily along the dirt road, and the dust was irritating his eyes and the back of his throat.

An old man with one blind eye was watching him steadily with the other one, without expression.

The mountain glowed enormous against a deep blue sky.

Stephen finished his counting, and realised with a shock what day it was.

April 20th. Thursday. The first day of school.

They would all be there now, in their sports jackets and blue ties, hair fresh cut for the new term. Strychnine. Potter. Soames. Mr Husting and Mr Wortle. But not him. He was Absent Without Leave. Gone missing. Would they ever have him back? Would he be expelled in his absence?

The enormity of what he had done suddenly struck him. Till now, he had never missed a prep or chapel. He had always obeyed the prefects and the masters, avoided getting into trouble of any sort. And now...

For better or for worse, it was too late now.

And he'd rather be here than there, any day.

'You're a perv, aren't you, Wiston?'

Stephen didn't answer.

Soames had come into his room unasked. He often did. Soames had a big body and a face like a fish. He was a year older than Stephen, and when he had nothing better to do he took a pleasure in mild torment.

'Your brother was a perv too. Come to a bad end, hasn't he? Just like you will.'

Stephen still didn't answer. Soames was too stupid to be worth that.

'What about all these pervy books then?' Soames started running his finger along Stephen's bookshelf. He pulled out a volume of Yeats' poetry that Mr Wortle had lent him. Soames immediately found the name inside the cover.

'Charles Wortle, eh? The man himself – the Wart – the arch-perv. That's what you do together, is it? Reading poetry. I'll bet!' He flicked through the pages and started reading aloud:

> *That is no country for old men. The young*
> *in one another's arms...*

110

Yuk! Disgusting!'

Stephen grabbed the book off him. Suddenly he was furious.

'Get out of my room, Soames, and if you want to know what's disgusting take a look in the mirror sometime. There's moss growing out of your nose.'

'No need to get personal,' said Soames, backing away.

In the autumn term the Junior Poetry Group was disbanded, and Stephen and Strychnine were invited to join the 'Aesthetes', a poetry society that met in the evening in Mr Wortle's room. The meetings were lively and funny and most of the members were sixth formers. These were some of the brightest boys in the school, Stephen realised, and although he was the youngest, he felt at home in the group. After one evening, one of the older boys approached him.

'I remember your brother,' he said. 'He was great. A breath of fresh air. I was younger than him, but God we used to laugh. Do you know where he is?'

'Not really,' said Stephen.

'Got away, has he? Lucky sod! I wish I had the guts to do what he did.'

There was fine weather early in the term. Mr Wortle invited Stephen and Strychnine to come for a trip to Oxford where they went punting on the river. Mr Wortle took photos of the boys stripped to their waists as they tried their hands at pushing the punts with long poles.

Stephen and Strychnine only managed to go in circles at first, causing a number of minor accidents, but fortunately Mr Wortle was an experienced punter.

'Did you go to Oxford, Sir?' asked Strychnine.

'Oh yes, indeed I did. Many years ago of course. Golden days. Those were golden days...'

'Bet it's not that long ago, Sir,' said Stephen.

Mr Wortle looked at him quickly.

'You're right, I'm still young – at heart, anyway.'

He launched into some Dylan Thomas:

'*Now as I was young and easy under the apple boughs*

About the lilting house and happy as the grass was green...

Youth – what a wonderful thing – such a pity it's wasted on the young!'

Stephen laughed. Mr Wortle seemed wonderfully witty.

They picnicked on a meadow in front of a pub, among groups of undergraduates – girls with clever faces, and boys with hair growing over their collars. It felt the height of sophistication to Stephen. They laughed and they talked and all three were in high spirits. School was forgotten.

He wanted the day to last forever.

Punting downstream was easier. Stephen and Strychnine both had another go, and were rather more successful this time, until Strychnine's pole got stuck, and the punt went on, leaving Strychnine hanging onto his pole, his lanky body flapping hopelessly as it subsided into the water. Stephen was laughing so much, he almost capsized the punt.

'Lucky I told you to bring spare clothes,' said Mr

Wortle. 'You *did* bring spare clothes, didn't you?'

They had.

'In that case, let's round off a perfect day with a cream tea.'

'Well,' commented Mr Wortle as he drove them back to Grindlesham. 'All things must pass. Back to reality.'

He sounded unhappy about it, too.

The villages were poorer and less frequent. The country was dry and thorny, and the sun was hot. Mount Ararat grew smaller behind them and the truck slowly emptied. At last it came to a halt and the last passengers took their chickens and wandered off on goat tracks into the wilderness. The driver climbed out of his cab and gestured at Stephen and Mary to get down.

'What do we do?' asked Stephen.

'We get out,' said Mary.

'But where on earth are we?'

Stephen looked around him at the moonlike landscape. Ararat hung spectrally in the distance behind them, and the plain stretched out towards some dusty hills.

'There was a sign a few miles back and I think it was saying we were approaching the border. I think we're nearly there. Let's hope!' said Mary.

They climbed down with their rucksacks. The boy assistant grinned.

'Iran!' he said, pointing down the road. Then with a last triumphant effort, 'Goodbye!'

The truck turned and rumbled back the way they'd come, leaving a cloud of dust.

It was actually good to be out of the truck with all its noise and dust. What from a vehicle had seemed an arid plain, was surprisingly beautiful when you were in it. The hills were streaked with amber and red, and among the stones and thorns beside the road grew purple orchids.

From somewhere, perhaps miles away, Stephen could hear a lark singing.

There was very little traffic. After half an hour, as they approached the hills, three Mercedes cars swished past them. Then a large truck with German plates came the other way. That was all.

They reached the hills, and the road turned and descended sharply. They went round one bend, then a second, and below them they saw the white painted concrete of the border post. Vehicles were parked in the compound, and guards lounged in a lookout. Below that, the road wound on down to a violet haze:

Iran.

There was a VW bus in the compound. Its owner was arguing with the customs officers, while its half dozen occupants spilled out of it like a colourful flock of exotic birds, reading, smoking, strumming guitar, or just sitting. Stephen and Mary had seen few Westerners since leaving Istanbul, and it was a welcome sight.

'Hi!' An American girl greeted them. 'Which way are you heading?'

Stephen and Mary slid their rucksacks off and sat down.

'East,' said Mary

'Oh, we're going the other way. Hey, this is one hell of a journey. How long did it take you to get from Istanbul?

'About five days,' said Mary. 'You can do it a bit quicker if you take the all-night express buses, but we took the train a lot of the way.'

'FIVE DAYS? You mean it's still five days of this?' She gestured at the empty country around her. 'Heck, I thought we were nearly there. Hey, Hans, these guys say it's another five days' travel.'

Hans was tall, with long hair under an embroidered hat, and loose colourful clothes. There was an authority about him that made Stephen slightly nervous. He smiled and sat down with them.

'You go on your own, just with the local buses? That's brave, but a good way to go. We take the easy way back – that is, if the van gets there. But when I came, I came like you. Is good, huh, when everything is new? I think Turkey is the hardest travel. Iran, Afghanistan, they are dangerous sometimes maybe, but you find good places to stay, where people tell you where to go next. It's getting like a big road. There will be a name for it soon. Back in Europe they will probably call it the Hippy Trail – something stupid like that!'

He laughed, turning to Mary.

'So what brings you East?'

'I want to see everything. The whole world, you understand?'

Hans nodded in agreement.

115

'There is no better reason to be alive.' He turned to Stephen. 'And you?'

'I'm looking for my brother,' said Stephen.

Hans raised an eyebrow. 'Well! We are all looking for our brother in a way. I hope you find him.'

'What about you?' asked Mary. 'Are you going home?'

'Home? I don't know what home is any more, but I am going West, back to the so-called civilisation, to see what is there for me. Sometimes I think it is the stupidest thing I can ever do. You know, it is tough in the East sometimes. I have dysentery now since three months. Often there is not enough to eat, and there are the bed-bugs and the rip-off merchants, but you are alive. You understand? Alive! Not like the half-dead zombies of our Western world.'

He paused, smiling gently at Stephen. His brown eyes were flecked with gold and sparkled with life.

'In Benares I met a Sadhu – a holy man – and he have change my life completely. He tell me to go back West, so I go, because I trust him. You must have trust. You will find your brother, if you have trust. Or if not your brother, then something else, something maybe more important.'

The van's owner had finished his argument with the customs. He brandished a clutch of passports and shouted over.

'Time to go!' said Hans. 'Good luck, guys! See you somewhere in this great wide world of ours!'

Chapter 11

Stephen woke up slowly, unsure for a while where he was. It was often like that now. So many towns. So many hotels.

A brilliant ray of sunshine came in through the little barred window, lighting up Carl and his brother Andreas, who were sitting on the end of his bed. Why on his bed? Because of the sunshine probably, but he didn't care anyway. They could sit on his bed if they wanted. He and Mary had met them at a bus station, and they'd travelled together through the desert, marvelling at the nomad camps and the camel trains. Now they were all sharing a four-bedded room, to save money.

Carl was giving Andreas a fix. He sucked an ampoule of morphine into a syringe, then pressed it till a drop appeared at the end of the needle. He had already put a tourniquet on Andreas' arm to pump up the veins, and he expertly slid the needle in. Andreas sat flushed and excited.

'You feel the rush?' asked Carl, in English for some reason, although they were both Austrian.

Andreas didn't need to answer. His eyes were glazing over. He was younger than Carl – younger than Stephen too, probably. He was a simple boy with a round pink face that he didn't need to shave. Carl had explained that he had gone all the way back to Vienna from India to fetch Andreas, because his life at home with his parents was so awful.

'He is my brother. So I look after him now,' said Carl. Which he did, in his own way.

Stephen started to sit up, and then flopped back again.

He knew where he was, now. The Hotel Bahram in Tabriz. A place with clean rooms and a garden, where warm evenings were filled with laughter and the smell of hashish. A place where Western travellers through Iran paused for a few days to recover. A place where junkies sat on the end of your bed fixing up in the morning sunshine.

'This is life,' he thought. 'This is real life, and I am in it.'

His home flashed into his mind. His mother, straightening his tie before she took him to church. She was forever straightening his clothes, pulling and patting, as if she was ashamed of how he looked. If she could see him now!

'Ja!' murmured Andreas, his face flushing and softening as the drug took hold. It was still new to him. 'Ja . . .' Carl was dismantling the syringe and wiping the needle.

Stephen sat up again, more awake now.

'Would you guys mind letting me have my bed back?' he asked.

'Sure,' said Carl. He and Andreas moved back to their own beds and lay down.

There was no sign of Mary. She must have already gone out. Reluctantly, Stephen edged himself out of his sleeping bag and slipped on his sandals. He had to go to the toilet. There was no avoiding it any longer.

The toilet was a stinking, shit-encrusted hole with elephants' feet to stand on as you squatted, and a rusty tin of water to wash your bum. Nobody ever used toilet paper, which you couldn't even buy from the shops. Like just about everybody else in the hotel, Stephen had chronic dysentery.

When he came out he stopped and looked at his face in the little scratched mirror that hung by the washbasin. He liked what he saw. He had lost weight, and his face had grown thinner and sprouted some soft down – you couldn't quite call it a beard – but his skin looked clear apart from a few insect bites, and his eyes were bright.

He owed a lot to Mary. She always made sure they ate well, and found good cheap restaurants. He wondered where she was now – probably in the market buying fruit.

Well, he couldn't wait around for her all day. He decided to go out and explore the bazaar.

It was already hot. After the mountains of Turkey it was a pleasant contrast, to wear a tee-shirt and his floppy hat, and feel the sweat breaking out on his back. He walked for a while down a smart modern avenue, and then turned into the ancient cramped alleyways that led to the old bazaar.

He had started at the wrong end – this was where the meat was sold, and he found it unpleasant. He walked past rows of fly-covered carcasses, and tethered goats waiting for the knife.

It stank and he hurried on through.

Perhaps he was moving too fast, because people were noticing him more than usual. Nobody spoke to him, but they stopped what they were doing and stared at him. A group of small boys who were poking in a bucket of innards, abandoned it and started to follow him.

Even in the shade of the alleys it was hot. The flies seemed to rise in clouds from the carcasses as he approached, and buzzed his face. He turned this way and that, trying to get out of the butchers' quarter, and had soon lost his sense of direction, but at last he came to the covered part of the bazaar, and the more congenial atmosphere of silversmiths and cloth shops.

The boys were still following him though. In fact they had gathered more, and become a pack. Stephen felt more confident now, and turned to face them, taking off his hat and bowing. He meant it as a joke, but they stepped back as if they were frightened for a moment. They didn't smile back as he had expected, just watched him with mouths slightly open, as if he was a rare beast, or an alien.

'Go away! ' he said, making a shooing gesture.

They obviously didn't understand, and wouldn't have gone if they had. So he did a little dance. Perhaps they would start to like him if he entertained them.

It was a mistake. The crowd grew bigger, but not more friendly.

He set off down the maze of streets, expecting the crowd to disperse, but they followed hot on his heels. When he stopped, they stopped. When he hurried, they hurried. The shopkeepers in the bazaar laughed and shouted comments.

'Hey Americaan!' shouted one of them. 'Coming my

shop!' and he made a gesture suggestive of smoking a hookah.

Stephen kept going.

There was a little group of boys at the front, bolder than the rest. They picked up the shopkeeper's refrain.

'Americaan!' they shouted at him. 'Americaan!'

He turned again and faced them.

'Not American. English!' he replied. It sounded stupid even to him, and the only effect on the boys was to encourage them. A youth at the back of the crowd shouted something he couldn't understand, but it wasn't friendly.

He had to get out, out of these little streets, back into the open, back to his hotel.

He turned and ran.

The boys ran after him.

He had no idea where he was, so he ran at random, and after him ran the children, more excited by the minute, until the bazaar petered out and he found himself in a blind alley with high walls all around him.

He stopped, because he had no choice. The alley behind him was a sea of small faces.

He took a step forward, wondering if he could push through.

'Let me through!' he said stupidly in English.

The crowd pulled tighter together.

'Americaan!' they shouted back. 'Americaan!'

He felt something hit him in the shoulder. Then something pinged off the wall behind him. Then his face . . .

They were stoning him.

He hadn't expected this. There had always been crowds, staring, jostling, trying to sell him things, but he had always felt they meant no harm, until now. What did they see that was so terrible in him that they wanted to stone him? They seemed to think he was American – did they hate Americans, or all foreigners, even? He knew nothing about politics. Perhaps it was his hat, like Mary said. He took it off and looked round the faces. The children at the front shrank back a fraction. They hadn't picked up stones, yet, but their faces were tight with anticipation. He might as well have been a cat, or a lizard.

There was another shower of stones, hitting him in the stomach, the shoulder, bouncing off the wall.

A tremor of fear ran up Stephen's spine. They might kill him, if nobody stopped them. There was no escape.

He bunched his fists. He couldn't just stand there. He would fight if he had to. The crowd liked him bunching his fists. Some of the boys bunched theirs back at him.

Another stone hit him on the shoulder.

A boy of about eleven was forcing his way to the front. He broke through, and looked up urgently at Stephen.

'Come! This way!' he said in English, beckoning.

There was a small door in the wall. In his fear, Stephen had hardly even noticed it. The boy pushed it open, and in a moment Stephen was through. The boy slammed the door behind him and slid across a thick wooden bolt. Already, the crowd was thumping on the door from the other side.

The boy grinned up at him.

'Lucky!' he said. 'This my house! Very safe!'

They were in a courtyard, with a fountain and blossoming fruit trees. On a divan in front of the fountain a middle-aged man was reading a newspaper. He looked up puzzled for a moment, and the boy ran over to him and talked excitedly, then he came over to Stephen, his arms extended, smiling.

'Welcome,' he said. 'From which country?'

'England,' Stephen answered, wondering where he was and what was happening. He could still hear shouting from the street.

'England? Very nice country. I am happy to meet you.'

The man shook his hand warmly.

'What is your name?'

'Stephen.'

'How do you do? My name is Mehmed, and this is my son, Asif. Please come inside. Meet my wife and daughters.'

He led Stephen into the house, which was cool and comfortable with rich carpets.

'This is Parveneh. And this is Mitra. And my little darling, Darya.'

Darya was a sweet six-year-old, but the other two girls were older, beautiful and sophisticated. They smiled at Stephen and shook his hand.

'Sit down! Sit down, please! My wife will bring tea and sweets.'

'Are you from England?' asked Parveneh, the eldest

123

girl. 'I would so much like to go there sometime. You must tell us about it.'

Stephen realised he had hardly even seen a girl apart from Mary since he had left Istanbul. Parveneh and Mitra had sleek black hair and huge dark eyes, and they were also relaxed, charming and spoke excellent English. He sat with them, his chest still thumping with adrenaline, trying to make conversation about his home, while their mother brought delicious sweets made with dates and coconut, and little Darya stared at him wide-eyed.

'So what has brought you to Iran?' asked Mitra. 'We don't see so many foreigners in our country.'

For a moment, Stephen didn't know what to say. What had brought him? And how could he put it in a way that they would understand?

'It's my brother,' he said. 'He left home and I have to find him, to make sure he is all right. I think he is in Afghanistan.'

'Why did he leave home?' asked Parveneh.

'I don't know,' said Stephen. 'But I think he was just looking for adventure.'

The girls smiled, understanding.

'That's how it's always been,' said Mitra. 'You and your brother, you are like heroes from one of our stories. Seeking for your lost brother – it is so romantic.'

'What about you?' asked Stephen. 'I mean, do you study or anything?'

'Oh yes!' said Parveneh. 'Mitra will be a writer, but I study to be doctor. Then I like to travel also. Perhaps I can

124

go to your country. Do you have television in your house?'

They talked and they ate, and in the meantime a policeman came in and Mehmed and Asif led him through the courtyard and out into the alley. But nobody mentioned the hostile crowd or the stone-throwing, or Stephen's foolishness. In this charmed and beautiful space, how could all that have existed?

Mehmed came over, with a wide smile.

'And now,' he said, pulling on a pair of white gloves, 'I will do some magic!'

'I don't believe you,' said Mary. 'I mean, I believe you could get yourself chased, but not the rest of it.'

'I'll take you to the house,' said Stephen. 'They want to see you. I told them about you and they asked us to come and have a meal with them tomorrow evening – but you'll have to watch the old man's conjuring tricks. They're quite good, actually. But Mary, why did those boys chase me? I hadn't done anything.'

'You made a spectacle of yourself,' said Mary. 'That's enough here. I'd have thought you'd have realised that by now. But we don't know, really. Perhaps they thought you were an American and they don't like Americans, or maybe they didn't really see you as anything – not human, you know. It happens. Black people get treated like that in the West sometimes. But you'll never know. That's the thing here, you don't know what's going on, you're only guessing.'

Stephen lay back on his bed reading *The Catcher in the Rye*, which reminded him of his school. He didn't want to be reminded of his school, so he put it down and shut his eyes for a moment.

Carl and Andreas had gone out, so he and Mary had the room to themselves.

Mary came over to his bed and sat beside him. She put out a hand and touched his hair.

'Your hair's growing.'

'I know.'

She carried on stroking it gently, looking at him quizzically. Stephen was paralysed. He had no idea what he was supposed to do. It wasn't that it was unpleasant, but it made him afraid – more afraid in a way than he had been in the alley that afternoon.

What did she want from him?

'Stephen,' she said.

'Yes . . . ?'

'Did you ever have a girlfriend, at home?'

'Not really. I was at a boys' school. I didn't meet a lot of girls.'

'Are you interested in girls, at all? I mean, sexually.'

'Yes, of course I am. At least . . .'

Finally he looked up and caught her eye. She leant forward, and kissed him gently on the mouth. He felt himself responding, and he put his arms round her, feeling the strength of her small back, pulling her towards him. He could smell her sweat, and feel the pulse of her body against his. He wanted to kiss her, he wanted to be part of her. His lips found hers again...she closed her eyes and ran her fingers along his neck.

Along his neck...It was like a knife cutting him. Cutting at the root of his feeling. He gasped, and moved his head away.

'What's the matter?'

'I don't know. I don't know what it is. It's something in me...I just can't...'

Mary stood up. She was upset, and her voice was hard.

'What is it about you, Stephen? I thought at first you might be queer what with your public school and all that, but you're not, are you? There's something you're not telling me though, isn't there? Well, you don't have to.'

'I want to,' said Stephen. 'I want to, Mary. I've never had a friend like you, Mary. I think you're amazing. It's just that...'

'Just what?'

What could he say? That she wasn't Astrid? Or that the way she stroked his neck had reminded him of Mr Wortle?

He breathed deeply.

'Mary, can we just be friends? I don't think I can handle any more than that, not at the moment.'

'Have it your own way,' she said. She collected her bag and went out.

Stephen lay back on his bed. He was shaking.

Mr Wortle. Walking down the colonnade in a paisley cravat, smiling.

127

'Ah Wiston, just the fellow I was looking for. Are you doing anything this Saturday?'

'No, Sir.'

'Then why not come up to my rooms for a little get-together? We'll have a little, er, refreshment. An evening of Romantic Poetry, I thought. You and a couple of others. *Crème de la crème*, you understand?'

Soames happened to walk past at that moment. He stretched his long ugly face into a look of disdain.

'What time, Sir?'

'Oh, not too late. About eight o'clock I should say.'

When Stephen arrived in his rooms, there were candles and white German wine, and a record of John Gielgud reading Keats' odes. But there were no other boys.

'They couldn't make it, dear boy,' said Mr Wortle. 'Never mind, we can enjoy ourselves without them...'

Stephen woke up suddenly, a full moon shining straight through the window. He lay wide awake, thinking about his father.

He had loved him so much, once. When he was small, his father had been a figure of romance, coming back on leave from Aden, tanned and strange, with exotic presents, taking his sons out to the zoo, or for walks on the hills. Those visits had been something Stephen longed for.

But he couldn't touch his children, even then. He couldn't take them on his knee and cuddle them while he read them a story – instead he would perch on the end of the bed, safely out of range. Sometimes he would pat

Stephen on the head – that was as far as it went, apart from a formal handshake when he said goodbye.

Remembering, a rush of longing went through Stephen, a great ache for his father, a great need to show his love, and the impossibility of ever doing so. He imagined his father dying, and trying to tell him how much he loved him. But he couldn't. It wouldn't come out. Even in his imagination, it just wouldn't come out.

Touch and love, they went together somehow. To love and not touch, it did something to you, it curled you up inside.

He was like his father, he realised. Perhaps in more ways than he ever knew.

Chapter 12

One hotel to another. One bus to another. They were merging into Stephen's consciousness now, just a backdrop to The Journey, that confronted him every day with something completely new, completely unexpected, and inexplicable: nomad camps of brown flat tents with vast herds of goats chewing thorns, and camel trains through the desert, and children of incredible beauty in lights such as he had never seen in Europe, and old men smoking hookahs at roadside halts, squatting in the dust with perfect ease. Lives of simplicity and dignity alongside the poverty and hustle of the shoe-shine boys, the soft drinks sellers, the vendors of trinkets pushing for a few coins off a rare Western tourist before he disappeared again out of their lives for ever.

This was a journey in time, as well as space. The centuries rolled back outside the bus window, back to the middle ages, to the Old Testament.

Sometimes his home felt so far away, he had almost forgotten his former self, felt that he could be anyone he wanted here, could forget his own name and make up another. At other times, the past welled up inside him with such power that he forgot the present.

It was dangerous here, he knew that. There was always danger here for a traveller and a non-Muslim. Talking to people, he began to understand a little of the politics. On the surface Iran was an orderly country, run by its king –

the Shah – with ruthless efficiency and ample oil revenues. Teheran was overwhelmed with Western goods and as thick with traffic as Istanbul. But there was an edge, always an edge. It didn't take much to realise that the Shah was loathed by the people, along with his secret police and his American backers. In the Amir Kabir Hotel in Teheran, where the foreigners gathered to smoke hashish round the fountain, there were ferocious tales of bandits and fanatics, of Westerners being raped, murdered or mutilated. Stephen had thrown away his green hat, and wore a scarf tied round his head against the sun, which attracted less attention. But any foreigner – even Mary – stood out here, and whenever they stopped a crowd gathered that was not necessarily friendly.

Most of the foreigners they met smoked hash, although it was illegal and the penalties severe. But the atmosphere was calmer in Teheran than in Istanbul, and they weren't disturbed in the hotels. In the courtyard of the Amir Kabir, joints and chillums passed freely, but Stephen never smoked them, mainly from habit, but also because the input to his senses was enough already.

Days had passed, weeks even. A few days' bus rides, Mary had said, but it was far beyond that. Sitting on the bus to Meshed, in Eastern Iran, Stephen once again tried to count the days since he'd left, but he kept ending up with different figures. He no longer knew the day of the month, or the day of the week. He was passing out of the known, into a reality where time had a different meaning.

Everywhere, there were mosques, and mullahs with

their black turbans and stern faces. Iranian mosques were very different from the Turkish ones, with short stout minarets and brilliant blue and green tiles covered in floral or geometric designs, or verses from the Koran. The call of the muezzin was much the same though, crackling through loudspeakers five times a day, and the devotion of the people was if anything even greater. When he had the opportunity, Stephen would go in and sit quietly absorbing the atmosphere. Mary never joined him.

'I've had enough of religions,' she said. 'They make nothing but trouble. Anyway you don't know what it's all about. You don't have a clue, do you?'

'No, I don't,' Stephen admitted, 'but I like sitting there. There's a peace.'

Stephen had read all the books he brought with him, and given them away, so he returned to the one Jerry had lent him: *Journey to the East*. As the bus bumped its way through the Salt Desert of Eastern Iran, he realised he had understood almost nothing of it on his first reading. The Journey to the East was not really an outer journey at all. It was a journey inwards, into the mind. Or perhaps the two were the same...

It made him wonder about his own journey. What was it that kept drawing him on into ever stranger places? He was looking for Rob. Yes, of course he was. But there was more to it than that. He flicked back to the blank page where he had pencilled in '*Reasons for trying to find Rob*' in the British Consulate, long ago, it seemed. None of them were really about Rob, were they? They were all to do with himself. It was himself he had to find, not his brother. No, it was both, and the two could never be separated.

For our goal was not only the East, Hesse wrote, *or rather the East was not only a country and something geographical, but it was the home and youth of the soul, it was everywhere and nowhere, it was the union of all times.*

The union of all times... Stephen considered that as Mary slept, her head lolling towards his shoulder: the biblical landscape outside the window; the bits of poems and books in his head, the accumulated knowledge of a twentieth-century Western education; and then the crowded bus on the dirt road, the timeless faces of the passengers, a mother nursing her baby, the driver at this moment shouting something at the conductor; and all mixing up with the memories of the life he'd left behind, that suddenly shook him with super-real clarity.

The union of all times – yes he could glimpse that. But *the home and youth of the soul* – what did that mean?

Soon they would be in Meshed, the last city before the Afghan border. Afghanistan. Another country. 'A country of the mind' someone had called it. What did that mean?

The bus stopped, as it often did, to let in a family, who squatted in the aisle as there weren't any seats left. The baby cried and the woman fed it. All over the world, life was going on, just as it was here. Everybody locked up in their own little bubble that they called reality, everybody with their own little goals, their own quiet desperations. Like Stephen's mother. Or Carl the junkie and his brother. Or the beggar woman at the bus station in the last town, carrying a tiny baby, with her extraordinary radiant beauty and desperate eyes as she held up a hand to Stephen, begging. What was her story, he wondered? What harshness, what courage, what betrayal, what love and desire had shaped her life? Suddenly he wanted to know all the stories of everyone, all over the world. A mountain of stories, to crush his own to insignificance.

The bus changed down a gear, and slowed. They were going up into the mountains again. The conductor and the driver were still arguing. Next to him, Mary adjusted herself to a more comfortable position.

Stephen thought of the family that had saved him from stoning. He had gone back there with Mary, already wondering if the house existed, whether it had been a hallucination. But they had been warmly welcomed, and the girls had made a fuss of Mary and braided her hair, and Asif and Darya had shown them how they made carpets, on a loom where any member of the family with an idle half hour could go and sit and tie the tiny knots. They had drunk tea and eaten fragrant rice in the evening light by the fountain, while the father did conjuring tricks, and Stephen had shown Mary the little door that had been his escape route – though none of the family ever mentioned the incident again.

And yet already, it was as if it had never been, as if it was a story from a half-forgotten book, or a dream.

When he was back, perhaps the whole journey would seem like that.

It did already.

Martin – the boy who had been arrested at the Turkish border; Stephen had met him again in Teheran. People seemed to keep cropping up here when you least expected them. Martin wanted to borrow a dollar, to get to Afghanistan.

'I pay you back in Kabul. I get money there and pay you back for sure.'

It didn't seem likely, and Stephen was reluctant to give up any of the precious bundle of notes he had got from selling Jerry's hash, but he found it impossible to refuse.

'Okay,' he said. 'But I'll need it back. I haven't got a lot left myself.'

'Sure I give it you back,' said Martin. 'You like drink a Coke?'

'Okay. By the way, I keep wondering how you got out that time on the Turkish border. Did the guy just let you go?'

'He buggered me,' said Martin simply. 'That was what he wanted. No big deal. It happen all the time. Have nobody buggered you yet?'

'No,' said Stephen, blushing.

Beside him in the bus, Mary stirred, woke and leaned past him to peer out through the dust-smeared glass of the window.

'Where are we?'

Stephen laughed. It was a ridiculous question.

'On the bus!'

'I know that!' said Mary, snappishly. 'Why are we going so slowly?'

'We're going uphill,' said Stephen. 'It's another mountain range, I think. Maybe it'll be a bit cooler at the top.'

'Well, I hope we stop for a break soon. I need a pee.'

At least the road was better. For no obvious reason, the crushed stone surface had upgraded to tarmac, so it was less dusty as well as less bumpy. Out of the window they could see thorns and shrubs among the rocks. They were climbing quite steeply now, zigzagging up a slope. There was no river at the bottom, just a dried up water-course, but there was a mud-covered village at a distance from the road, with a few trees.

Mary yawned.

'What's the time?'

Stephen pulled his watch out of his waistcoat pocket. His grandfather's watch – he never wore it because it attracted attention, but he was glad he hadn't sold it, along with his suit and his shoes. He felt guilty about selling them too, but he couldn't have taken them.

'Five o'clock, nearly.'

'It'll be getting dark soon. I guess it's still a long way to Meshed. Why do we always have to arrive in new places at about two o'clock in the morning?'

The heat had gone out of the day already, and the light had softened. Soon it would be freezing cold, and though the bus did have some basic heating, Stephen was glad he'd bought a shawl in Teheran. He'd rolled it up to use as a pillow, so he unrolled it now and placed it round his shoulders. Most of their luggage was on top of the bus, safely roped down, they hoped. Stephen was never completely sure that his rucksack would still be there on arrival though, so he kept a small bag of essentials with him, as well as his money bag round his neck.

They were the only foreigners on the bus. It was usually like that – the Amir Kabir had been full of all sorts of Westerners – tough, bearded Australians making the overland trip to Europe; heavy smoking American GIs coming back from Vietnam the slow way, with a surface calm and freaked-out eyes; keen-eyed kids taking a year off before going to university; junkies heading for the morphine-fuelled paradise of Goa; hippies on the dope trail, semi-serious archaeologists, traders and adventurers. They'd all gathered in the same hotel, sharing hash and swapping stories. Some were driving as a group in vans like Jerry's, others took local transport. The really brave or really broke hitchhiked. It was one road, and people cropped up at unlikely moments, and met in friendly hotels the names of which were passed on like mantras. But outside the relative safety of the cities you were on your own, a total stranger in a land where the rules were unwritten and unknown, and the penalty for breaking them might easily be death.

You could just disappear here. No one would ever know.

They were near the top of the pass. Stephen could feel cool air coming through the window. It was pleasant.

The driver was singing, swerving the bus around the road. A truck came the other way, and they played the normal game of chicken – keeping to the middle, waiting to see who would blink first. At the last minute, the truck swerved, and they missed each other by inches. Below them a rocky hillside sloped steeply towards a gorge. The driver shouted out triumphantly, and the conductor yelled back at him, perhaps telling him what an idiot he had been.

The driver turned to argue, and took both his hands off the wheel. The bus was still going uphill, quite slowly.

The bus nudged the rock face and bounced back. It wasn't a hard impact, but enough to send the driver sprawling off his seat.

Everything seemed frozen. The driver was slithering on the floor, and the conductor was struggling to get to the steering wheel. A woman was screaming. In slow motion, the bus was heading for the edge of the road.

Mary gripped Stephen's arm.

'Oh my God! We're going over!'

The front wheels left the tarmac. The momentum was just enough to slide the bus forwards onto the steep slope, nose first, until the back came up and over in a huge somersault.

It bounced once, then slid a little way and came to rest, perched precariously against a boulder.

Stephen found himself sitting on the mountainside. The sun was shining full in his face, casting long shadows

138

among the rocks. Broken glass and luggage were scattered around him.

Some way below he could see the bus. The back wheels were still spinning.

For a few moments it was silent. Then a woman started to moan, a low, desperate groaning.

Stephen felt himself all over. His leg hurt, but he could move it. He stood up. He was bruised and shaken, but nothing seemed to be broken. He looked around and saw the bag that he'd had on the bus, and his shawl. He picked them up, almost absent-mindedly. A few yards away, an old man was raising his arms in the air and chanting a desperate prayer to the heavens.

Suddenly he remembered Mary. Where was she? The bus! She must be still in the bus. He had been next to the window, so he had been flung out, but Mary would have held on. He half ran, half slid down the hill, surprised how well his sore leg carried him.

The bus was in one piece and the right way up, but tilted at a strange angle. Stephen ran to the window where they had been sitting, and looked through where the glass had been. Mary was sitting in her seat, as if the bus had just pulled up. There was moaning and sobbing in the background. She looked down at Stephen, and smiled, as if from a long distance.

'Are you all right?'

'I think I'm fine,' she said, shakily. 'Let's see.'

She clambered out of the window, careful not to cut herself on the remaining shards of broken glass. He helped her down. She was being very careful with her left arm, and hung onto him for balance.

'Oh my God, we're still alive.'

Families were regrouping around them, searching for belongings among the debris. For a few moments, oblivious to everything else, Stephen and Mary stood on the hillside in the fading light and hugged each other. They shut their eyes and felt the world dissolve.

When they opened their eyes, a crowd had formed. A young man was pointing at them. He started shouting.

'What's happening?' asked Stephen.

'I don't think they like us,' said Mary. 'They're probably blaming us for what's happened. Because we're immoral heathen, as we've just proved. I think we'd better move.'

'What about our bags?'

'Forget the bags,' said Mary urgently, starting to climb the hill towards the road. 'Let's hope there's some help on the way.'

Behind them the young man seemed to be having an argument with an older man. The old man had authority, but it was the young man who had more support.

'Look!' Mary pointed at the road below them, where a vehicle was making its way up the hill. 'Let's get up to the road before that gets here. You never know, it might be friendly!'

They hurried on. Below them, a group of younger men separated from the others, and were following them, moving with a good deal more agility than they were. They clambered up the hill, through the scattered contents of burst open luggage from the top of the bus. Improbably, Stephen spotted the photo of his parents, smiling wanly from beside a rock. He didn't dare pause to look further, but he plucked it as he passed and pushed it into his passport bag.

They reached the road, and stood there, not sure what to do. They'd lost sight of the vehicle, though they could still hear its motor.

'Let's hope it's not full of fanatics,' muttered Mary.

The men caught up with them, and then stopped a few yards away, as if they weren't sure what to do either. Mary and Stephen turned to face them, backing slowly away down the road. Mary pulled her scarf across her mouth.

The men walked towards them. There was anger in their faces, but they were unsure too. Suddenly one of them – the same young man who had pointed at them – erupted with shouts, pointing upwards to the sky, and then at Stephen and Mary. He was actually crying, Stephen saw. Perhaps one of his family had been killed or injured. His comrades put their arms round him, comforting him.

'You'll have to handle this,' said Mary from behind her scarf. 'Don't turn your back, whatever you do. And don't show you're frightened.'

Oddly, Stephen wasn't frightened. He knew he should have been, but he wasn't. His heart was beating hard, but his breath was steady and his head was clear.

He stopped, and let his hands fall to his sides.

'We haven't done anything,' he said in English, as calmly as he could. No one could have understood the

141

language, but they knew what he meant. They kept advancing, but more slowly.

'We didn't do anything,' he said again, calmly. Mary was behind him, hiding her face. Stephen tried to look in the eyes of as many of the men as possible – there were seven of them, most of them young. They had all just been through the same bus crash. Every face showed deep emotion.

'You should go back and look after your people,' Stephen said. 'It wasn't our fault.'

Their leader started to shout again. He went on his knees and banged the tarmac with his palms – was he praying? The men behind him muttered their support for him.

But they came no closer.

The sound of the engine was suddenly louder. Stephen glanced over his shoulder as it came into view round the bend. The sun was shining in his eyes, half blinding him, but it looked like a van or small bus. It might even be foreign.

But he kept facing the men. He needed to look them in the eyes – all of them. For some reason he was convinced they couldn't kill him if he looked them in the eyes.

The van slowed right down as it approached, but without stopping. A man's voice shouted, 'Get in!' in English, and Mary yelled, 'Run!'

At that moment a blast of fear hit Stephen. They were going to kill him. He knew it. He couldn't move. His legs had turned to jelly. The leader of the group sprang forward towards him.

'Stephen!' yelled Mary.

She grabbed him, and as the van came level, bundled him in front of her through the side door. As she slammed the door shut, fists hammered against it, and angry voices hurled abuse. The van picked up speed and drove on.

Stephen lay panting on the floor, his eyes closed. Only slowly did he take in where he was.

He was back in the Green Bus – Jerry's van. The man driving it was Reuben, and Jerry was leaning backwards over the passenger seat to talk to them. He had grown a moustache.

'Hi, Stephen!' said Jerry, grinning his lop-sided grin. 'Good to see you, man!'

Part 3:
A Country of the Mind

The air was full of dust and, as the sun set, everything was bathed in a blinding saffron light. There was not a house or a village anywhere, only a whitewashed tomb set on a hill and far up the river bed, picking their way across the grey shingle, a file of men and donkeys. Here for me, rightly or wrongly, was the beginning of Central Asia.

Eric Newby: *A Short Walk in the Hindu Kush*

Chapter 13

On the 29th April 1966, twenty-six days after Stephen had first met Jerry and Astrid on the ferry to France, he crossed the border into Afghanistan in the Green Bus.

He knew the date because of the stamps in his passport.

The border was a tree trunk hung across the road, and a soldier asleep in a tent in a flat wilderness. They moved the tree trunk themselves. The customs post was ten miles further on, in an oasis of mulberry trees, where tribesmen and police in ragged uniforms sat on string beds around a hookah.

The Green Bus was the only vehicle passing through that morning, and no one was in any hurry to deal with it. They sat on the verandah, waiting for the inspector, looking out past the mulberry trees at flat, cracked wastelands, and drinking fragrant tea served in floral china teapots.

When the inspector finally came, he stamped their passports without looking at them, then said sternly:

'You have hashish?'

'No,' said Jerry, automatically.

'No? NO??'

The inspector frowned, then shouted:

'Then you should have hashish! Here! I give you hashish! Take this one! Finest quality!'

He held out a fat brown lozenge of hash, and roared with laughter.

'Welcome to Afghanistan! The Country of the Free!'

Herat.

Nowhere had been like this.

A policeman in a battered topee stood on a timber platform at the main intersection, blowing a whistle at flocks of goats and horse-drawn carriages, or, very occasionally, at one of the five motor vehicles in the town.

In the evening, Stephen sat in a rose garden in front of the mosque, fragrant with the smell of roses and hashish, listening to the tinkle of harness and the clip-clop of hooves, while thousands of tiny white kites flew from the rooftops, pulled on invisible strings. A boy of about ten offered him a rose. A turbaned tribesman on a white horse stopped and stared, then saluted Stephen with a wide smile. Finches chattered in the bushes. He had not seen a television nor heard amplified sound in the whole city. Instead there was peace. Ancient, timeless peace.

At night there were thunderstorms. From his bedroom window Stephen watched the crenellated silhouette of the citadel lit with constant stroboscopic effects, while the thunder cracked and rumbled and the rain poured down. Every morning was fresh and perfect in the sunshine.

Stephen and Mary had parted company with Jerry and Reuben when they reached Herat. Jerry's idea was to stay in the suburbs in an ex-colonial hotel, which had a big fence and a private garden, but Mary wanted to go to the Bamian – a cheap hotel near the bazaar. Stephen was happy to separate. However grateful he was to Jerry and

Reuben for coming to their rescue, he had never managed to feel quite comfortable with them. The memory of the hash in his suitcase in Istanbul lay unspoken between them. Stephen had many times been on the point of raising the subject, but somehow couldn't bring himself to, and Jerry acted as if it had never happened.

Stephen did ask Jerry how he got out of prison, though.

'Hey, they only found a couple of grams; they couldn't pin a whole heap on me with that. Then Reuben turned up and passed some baksheesh, and I was out again. So we thought we'd come East – see where we get to. Lucky for you, huh? Those guys might've killed you, easy. No one would have ever known.'

Stephen shuddered. Jerry was right. Their bodies would have disappeared and no questions ever asked. It had been their fault in a way, though. It had been a serious mistake to embrace like that on the hillside, drawing attention to themselves at the worst moment. Yet Stephen also felt guilty about leaving the crashed bus, with people injured and possibly killed. Not that there was anything he could have done. He had been badly bruised himself, and Mary's wrist had swelled up, though she didn't complain or see a doctor.

From the moment Jerry rescued them, their main desire was to get out of Iran as quickly as possible, and they lay gratefully in the back of the Green Bus, reliving the crash in their minds, while Jerry and Reuben took turns in driving non-stop to the border.

Should he hate Jerry? Stephen wondered. Jerry had

deceived him and put him in enormous danger, and for a while in Istanbul Stephen had felt betrayed, but the reality of Jerry was strangely disarming. You just couldn't go on disliking him. Rob had that quality too, the ability to act selfishly and be forgiven.

'They're going to load up the van with hash and smuggle it back to Europe,' said Mary. 'That's what they've come for, it's obvious. Then Reuben'll get him busted somewhere, and that'll be Jerry's number up for the foreseeable future.'

'Do you think I should warn him?' asked Stephen. 'About Reuben I mean?'

Mary shrugged.

'Up to you.'

Since the night in the hotel in Iran, Stephen's relationship with Mary had ebbed and flowed. They spent so much time together, sitting in buses, sharing rooms, eating – and sometimes they were so close it felt as if they were thinking each other's thoughts. Then Mary would recoil from the closeness.

'I hardly know you,' she'd say. Then she'd tease him about his posh accent and his public school.

Sometimes he started to tell her about it – the school. But it was the one thing – the only thing – she didn't really seem to understand.

'You know what? Potter and Windham got caught smoking.'

'They didn't!'

'They did,' said Strychnine. 'They were behind the bogs having a fag, and Beaky Williams came round and caught them. He took them straight back to his office and beat them.'

'That's outrageous,' said Stephen.

'I don't see why. You always get beaten for smoking.'

'I know, but he didn't have to go out looking for them, did he? I mean if he'd just come across them by accident, that'd be different. But nobody goes behind the bogs by accident. He was just looking for them because he wanted to beat somebody. What an arsehole.'

Not like Mr Wortle. He never did things like that, sneaking round trying to catch boys out. He treated everybody with respect. That was what Stephen liked – the way he talked to him as an equal.

'Punishment's a complete waste of time, don't you think?' he had said to Stephen the night before, pouring him a glass of wine in his room. 'I mean, as a schoolmaster one goes through the motions because one has to be seen to be playing the game, but nobody ever became more intelligent or a better person by being beaten, or forced to write lines, or whatever. Besides, when something is forbidden, it only makes you want to do it more – in fact, the more dangerous, the more alluring. Like cannabis, for example. Have you ever smoked cannabis, Stephen?'

The question took him by surprise. All he knew about cannabis was some lurid reports in the newspaper.

'I thought it was really bad...like it drove you nuts and things...'

'Oh no, I'm sure it's quite harmless. It's not exactly new, you know. Certainly, European literature would be immeasurably poorer without it. Baudelaire, Rimbaud, Coleridge...It wasn't illegal of course, then. Kipling had supplies shipped out to him from India, and I believe Queen Victoria was rather keen on it too. No, I fear we live in prudish times, Stephen, when many of life's pleasures are banned, though no less delightful for that.'

'Would you take it yourself, Sir?' asked Stephen, emboldened by the wine.

'Ah...Well I can't very well admit to that now, can I? Who knows who you might tell...'

'I wouldn't tell anyone!' Stephen protested.

'Splendid!' said Mr Wortle. 'Have a drop more wine before you go. And perhaps we could get together again on Sunday afternoon. There's a gem of a Norman church down by Ilserford, that I'd like to show you. We could go out there in my car. Keep it under your hat, though. We wouldn't want any of your friends to get jealous!'

It felt good to be alone with Mary again, in a two-bedded room in the Bamian Hotel, with a view of the citadel.

Stephen spread out his remaining belongings on his bed. There was not much: the bus crash had left him only the clothes he was wearing – jeans, shirt, waistcoat – and the few bits and pieces in his shoulder bag: his school spongebag with toothbrush, soap and a flannel, spare pairs of socks and underpants, *Journey to the East*, his grandfather's watch (which had broken in the crash, and now always said five past five), a waterbottle, a stainless steel bowl and a spoon. That was it except for the money bag round his neck, with assorted documents and the wad of dollar bills Brian had given him for the hash. Living had been very cheap. The wad was still thick, though he would need to buy new clothes from it now.

He decided to sell his jeans and buy baggy Afghan trousers. He fancied the style. He might as well sell the watch too. Although it had stopped it was a good make and would be worth something, and was no use to him.

Mary had spread out her belongings on the other bed. She had even less than him.

'I miss my sleeping bag. It was a really good one – the only thing I had that was half decent. Nothing else though,' she said.

'You know that story in the Bible,' said Stephen. 'The one about it being easier for a camel to go through the eye of a needle than for a rich man to enter the Kingdom of Heaven?'

'What about it?'

'My divinity teacher told us that the eye of the needle was what they called a sentry gate, and that a camel could actually get through it, but only if it had nothing on its back, nothing attached to it.'

Mary laughed. 'That's us then. Kingdom of Heaven, here we come!'

Stephen lay back on his bed.

'Sometimes I think Herat *is* the Kingdom of Heaven,' he said.

He picked up *Journey to the East*, flicked through it, then flung it over to Mary, who caught it neatly.

'Here! Have this. It's Jerry's, but I don't suppose he wants it back yet. I've finished with it. It's quite good.'

He went downstairs to the restaurant and ordered tea and an omelette, with bread. The tea came in a china pot that had been glued back together several times, with a carefully crafted tin spout. There was so little in Herat – everything possible was recycled. The Afghanis seemed to live off greasy mutton stews that gave all foreigners dysentery, but the bread was wonderful – huge flat loaves fresh baked in the street in tandoori ovens, and given hot into your hands.

'Hey, Stephen!'

It was Carl. He was sitting with his brother, who had a happy, vacant expression. Probably he'd just had his fix. Stephen went over and joined them.

'You know, man, I hear something, you could be interested,' said Carl.

'What's that?' asked Stephen, without much interest. His omelette arrived and he tucked into it. He still had chronic diarrhoea, but it only made him hungrier.

'Yeah, about your brother. It's probably nothing, but there's some guys living out of town a bit, in some shrine there. They been long time in Afghanistan, man, long time in Kabul too, they know the scene here. Maybe they seen your brother.'

'Thanks, Carl,' said Stephen. It was a jolt to be reminded of Rob, though it didn't seem much of a lead. He had hardly thought about him recently, and given up asking about him. Most of the people he met in Herat were coming, as he was, from the West; the few coming the other way had mostly passed quickly through Kabul, anxious to get home. The last person he'd met who claimed to have seen Rob was the girl in Istanbul – it seemed a long time ago now.

'I meet one of them in the bazaar,' Carl continued, 'and I ask him if he know an English guy called Rob. He thought maybe, but his friend know him better. He say his friend know everyone.'

'Thanks, Carl,' said Stephen again, touched that Carl had gone to so much trouble for him.

'Is okay. I understand about looking for brothers,' said Carl, patting Andreas' leg and smiling at him affectionately.

'Where is this shrine then?' asked Stephen. 'How do I get there?'

A horse tonga took him out of town towards the barren hills to the north of the city. It stopped by an old mosque in a grove of dusty trees.

'*Inja!*' said the driver. 'Here!'

Stephen looked around apprehensively. The sky was implacably blue. Brown, empty hills stretched in every direction.

The tonga driver made a gesture to ask if he should wait. Stephen was worried about the expense, but he was more worried about being left on his own in this wilderness.

'*Bali*!' he nodded.

The tonga driver flicked his reins and the horse ambled on to the shade of an apricot tree.

Around the mosque were extensive ruins dotted with bushes and white-washed shrines, the burial places of Muslim holy men. A few low domed buildings were still intact, built of stone and mud and dug half into the ground. From one of these an old man emerged, dressed in white with an orange turban.

'*Assalaam aleikum*!' The old man greeted him with a slight bow.

'*Wa aleikume salaam*,' replied Stephen, enjoying the formal greeting.

The old man smiled and said something Stephen couldn't understand, then led him to the mosque. They paused and took off their sandals before entering. Inside, part of the dome had collapsed, revealing deep blue sky, but there was an elegant shrine and sarcophagus at one end, and Stephen understood at once that this was still a place of worship. He stood on the marble floor, watching some sparrows nesting in the dome and feeling the now familiar tingle through his body, while his guide prayed. Time seemed to slow down and the air about him was charged with prayer.

The old man finished his prayer, nodded at Stephen approvingly and asked, '*Farangi*?' (Foreigners?); then, without waiting for an answer, led him back out of the mosque and over some waste ground to a half submerged, white-washed building with a cracked dome. A large blue and brown bird cocked its head and watched him.

'*Inja! Inja!*' said the old man, beckoning him on. He went down some steps and pushed open a door.

Compared with the brilliant sunshine, it was dark inside, and Stephen could make out very little. An American voice called out:

'Hi there, man! Come on in and join us!'

The old man stepped aside, and Stephen went down the steps and into the room.

Four young Westerners were sitting on mats on the floor, their sleeping bags pushed back against the wall behind them, and some cooking pots in a corner. They moved to make a place for Stephen, and the American held out his hand and took Stephen's in a warm, firm clasp.

'Hi! I'm Bill. Welcome to our little piece of paradise!'

Bill had a big, friendly face and glistening eyes with very large pupils. Stephen appreciated the friendly welcome.

'I'm Stephen.'

'Good to see you, Stevie. You sound like you're English, so you're in good company here. Meet Gordon, Ian and Tony – they're all English.'

'No we're not,' said Gordon, rather crossly, 'I'm Scottish.'

'Yeah, Scottish,' said Bill, 'but that doesn't matter because one day they are going to go back home and take over the whole island, the whole damn caboodle – that's the plan, eh, Tony? Tony's gonna be the leader. We just decided.'

Tony was a boy with a young, attractive face and hair almost down to his waist, who at that moment breathed out a vast amount of smoke from a chillum he was holding, and slumped back against the wall, his mouth half open as if he was about to say something. His eyes revolved slowly, scanning the domed roof.

'It's – like – all – waves –' he said at last, with long pauses between each word. Then his eyes opened wide and he looked around brightly for a moment.

'The third wave!' he announced. 'That's it! The third wave!' He slumped back happily. Bill took the chillum off him.

'Third Reich more like,' muttered Ian, a skinny, clever-looking youth with round glasses and slightly shorter hair than the others.

'We've been planning the future of the planet,' drawled Bill. 'Now Ian here does not agree, and he has his reasons, which we respect, but the rest of us reckon that we guys are the good guys, so *we* have got to take over the planet, so's to make it a better place for everybody. And we *can* make it a better place, guys, we really *can*. We just have to dream our dreams and think big enough . . . Hey, Stevie, take a toke of this chillum, kid. We have got absolutely the best shit in Afghanistan here.'

'We'll never do anything if we don't sort out the basics first,' grumbled Gordon.

Bill ignored him.

'I'll show you how to hold it.' He pressed the chillum into Stephen's hand. 'You hold this damp cloth here, see, with your fingers – like that – and then cup with your left hand. That's it. You got it. The thing is, like that you don't ever have to touch the chillum with your lips. Some guy told me smoking is forbidden in the Koran, see, so if you don't touch the pipe with your lips, that makes it like not smoking. Jeez, I love that – it's not really smoking at all! You can get as stoned as you like – and we do! We do! And all you're doing is just breathing, and the smoke happens to be there! Far out!'

'Shut up, Bill, and let Stephen take a toke. Even shares for all, I say,' said Gordon, nodding at Stephen with one eye half closed, and what looked like a dour smile.

'The third wave!' Tony burbled happily, slumping lower, and making wavy motions with his hands.

'Actually,' said Stephen, 'I just came here to ask if any of you knew...'

'Chillum first, questions after,' said Gordon firmly.

Stephen looked down at the chillum. The crumbled hashish glowed red and a wisp of smoke tickled his nostrils.

He hesitated. Till now he had resisted all the offers of hash that had come his way, partly from fear, but mostly just out of habit. Mary smoked it in little joints sometimes, but she didn't even offer it to him any more.

Bill leaned over towards him, putting a friendly hand on his back and meeting his eyes.

'Hey, man, I can see it's your first go at a chillum, but relax, man. It'll be great. Go on! It'll take you places you've never been before!'

It was hard to resist, when Bill looked at him like that. He didn't want to be rude, when everyone was being so friendly. He would just take a little toke.

He held the chillum the way Bill had shown him, put it to his mouth and took a half-hearted drag. Nothing happened. He tightened his grip and dragged more strongly. This time the chillum flashed with fire and a cloud of smoke enveloped him. He fell back, spluttering and coughing.

'Nice one, Stevie,' said Bill affectionately, rubbing his back.

Stephen recovered from the coughing and held out the chillum, which Ian took. Apart from the coughing, the hash didn't seem to have had much effect. He felt calm and present. He looked round at everybody, smiling.

Tony had slumped further down the wall. His eyes were revolving slowly in different directions.

'How about a cup of tea?' suggested Gordon. 'Calming to the nerves.'

There was a samovar in one corner, an ornate silver urn with an oil lamp under it. Gordon poured tea from it into cracked china cups and passed them round. Stephen sipped his gratefully. It was bitter but refreshing to his dry throat.

That question he had come here to ask: what was it? It seemed to have slipped his mind just for now.

'How long have you guys been here?' he asked instead. His voice sounded distant, as if it was coming from someone else.

160

'Hey, that's a great question,' said Bill. 'How long we been here?' He puzzled for a moment. 'Sorry, you got me beat there, kid! Gordon'll tell you – he's good with figures – eh, Gord?'

'How long is a piece of string?' said Gordon, sitting down with his tea. 'Well, since you ask, seven days by conventional measurements, and seven centuries by the measurements of the great stoned Sufi sages.'

A crack in the roof of the dome let in a thin, brilliant sunbeam. Particles of dust danced in the sunbeam, pulsating vigorously when anyone moved. Stephen watched them, trying to follow a single particle for more than an instant, but he couldn't. All the same, he had never seen such a beautiful dance.

Ian passed the chillum to Bill.

'It's gone out.'

'Finished,' said Bill, tapping out the ash. He cleaned it slowly by rubbing a strip of cloth through it.

A long time passed. Possibly a very long time.

Stephen watched the sunbeam. It touched the top of Tony's head, making his hair glow golden.

Bill put a lump of chocolate-coloured hash into a small black bowl, and gazed at it.

Tony slid down onto the floor, and started to giggle uncontrollably. Gordon gave him a kick, and he stopped and pulled himself back up against the wall.

More time passed. Stephen became one with the sunbeam.

'Do you ever see God when you're stoned, Bill?'

Gordon asked, startling Stephen with his voice.

'Sure do,' said Bill, picking up the hash and sniffing it. 'I see Him all the time, stoned or not stoned, right here among us. He is in the trees and the rocks and the streams, the food we eat and the shit we shit. He is you and me and Tony and Ian, and Stevie here. He is even George. He is everywhere and He is all things.'

'Crap,' muttered Ian.

'I did see Him once, you know,' said Gordon pensively. 'It was the black Manali charas that did it. Face to Face, in all His Glory.'

'He is me! I am that!' announced Tony, and started giggling again.

'Crap!' said Ian again. 'Why do you all have to talk so much crap?'

'Because we're stoned,' said Bill, sensibly. 'Hey, loosen up, man. It's cool!' He lit two matches to heat the hash, then crumbled some into the bowl. He broke in tobacco from a cigarette, and worked the mixture together with his fingers.

The dance in the sunbeam had not changed in centuries, although it changed totally every moment...

A memory stirred in Stephen's brain...Something he had come here to ask. He couldn't immediately remember what it was, but he decided not to smoke another chillum, in case he got stoned.

He tried standing up. The dust particles danced furiously.

'I'm going outside for a bit,' he said.

'Far out,' said Bill.

'Nice idea,' said Gordon. 'I'd come with you, only we're hiding.'

'Hiding? Who from?'

'From George, of course. If you see him, for God's sake don't tell him we're here.'

'What does he look like?' asked Stephen, anxiously.

'You'll recognise him. Don't worry, he won't hurt you,' added Gordon considerately.

'Only, if you see any chicks, send 'em along,' said Bill. 'We sure need chicks!'

Tony, back on the floor, started clucking.

'Shut up, Tony,' said Bill, giving him a poke. 'You're pretty, but you're no chick.'

Stephen opened the door and blinked in the brilliant light. Bill, Ian, Gordon and Tony faded back into shadows.

As the door shut behind him he remembered what he was going to ask. Rob. That was it, Rob.

Who was Rob? What was Rob? Where was Rob? Why was Rob?

It could wait for now.

The blue and brown bird was looking at him from a rock. It tipped its head to one side and asked:

'Why are you here?'

Stephen couldn't answer that. He only knew he had come a long way to be there.

The bird flew towards the mosque and disappeared among some bushes. Stephen followed, gazing up at the tiles. They had looked interesting before, but now they were dramatic. Geometric patterns jumped and flashed at him like neon signs, Koranic verses in Arabic stood out in black against a blaze of fire.

It was more than he could handle. He lowered his gaze. Then he took off his sandals and went inside the mosque, thinking he would sit quietly in front of the shrine and collect his thoughts. But as he stepped through the doorway he saw a man – unmistakably an American, wearing a bomber jacket and jeans despite the heat. His hair was cut short, and his eyes were unusually close together.

It must be George.

'Hi there!' said George, heading towards Stephen with a broad smile, holding out his hand.

Stephen looked at George's feet. He was wearing patent leather shoes, just like the ones Stephen had sold in Istanbul.

'Shouldn't you take your shoes off?' asked Stephen. 'This *is* a mosque.'

'Dammit to hell!' The smile and the hand dropped. 'What are you? Some sort of Muzzy?'

'You wouldn't like it if someone came into a church wearing a hat,' Stephen pointed out.

'I ain't wearing no hat,' said George. 'Anyway this place is a wreck. Look at the state of it. Disgusting!'

Stephen looked around him. It was shady and cool – a relief after the bright sun – and though the tiles had fallen off in places, in others they glowed and danced while the birds fluttered in the dome. The lattice work around the

164

saint's tomb was crisp and clean, and the floor had been recently swept. Everywhere was steeped in deep, timeless peace. He had never been anywhere more beautiful.

'I'm looking for an American and three English guys,' said George. 'You seen them? I wanna find them. I'm gonna save their souls.'

'Why?'

'Whadya mean, why?'

He came up very close, and wagged his finger at Stephen's chest.

'I don't know about you, young man. I'm not sure I like your attitude. But you're young and you may learn, so take this from me: these people round here, these Afghanis, you don't want to mix with them. They got a lot of heathen ideas, because they don't read the Bible. And I don't like the way they treat their women either. Now I'm not saying it's their fault. Maybe they don't know better, and that's why I'm here, to give 'em a chance to learn a little civilisation from us, but if they don't, then sure as hell I'm going to teach 'em a lesson or two. Know what I mean? Now I want you guys with me, but if you guys can't see things straight, then you can be damned sure that I can, and I'll do what needs to be done, and I'll do it anyway. Because I got the power, see?'

He turned his back and walked out of the mosque. He had a funny way of walking, knees bent and feet angled outwards. As he left, a blob of birdshit landed on his head.

The peace closed back in behind him.

★

The tonga was still under the apricot tree. The old man emerged from the mosque again, raising his hand to bid Stephen farewell. Then at the last moment, Ian came running out of the ruins.

'Can I get a lift with you?' he asked.

'Of course.'

They drove off, back towards Herat.

Ian sighed.

'I couldn't take any more of that. I have to come down. Those guys are off their heads.'

The pony trotted sedately. The sun had dropped low in the sky, and light slanted through the pine trees lining the road. Children ran over to stare at them as they passed.

'I saw George, by the way,' said Stephen. 'He asked where you lot were, but I didn't tell him.'

'George?' asked Ian, puzzled. 'George?'

'George – you know, the guy you were hiding from.'

'Oh, *that* George! No, you can't have seen him. He doesn't exist. Bill and Gordon invented him. They dreamed up the most un-cool, ignorant, arrogant Westerner any of us could imagine, and then pretended we were escaping from him. It was a stoned fantasy, that's all.'

The horse clip-clopped along the road. There was a powerful scent of pine.

'I saw someone though,' said Stephen. 'He wore a bomber jacket and kept his shoes on in the mosque.'

'It does *sound* like George,' said Ian. 'Strange.'

They bumped gently on as the evening turned violet, and Stephen at last remembered the question he had gone there to ask. Perhaps it wasn't too late.

'Did you ever come across an English guy called Rob, who was in Kabul a few weeks ago?'

'Rob? Yes, I know someone called Rob. He has a chip on his tooth, just here. Looks a bit like you actually... Could be your brother.'

'He is,' said Stephen.

'Great! Well I hope *he* turns out to be real, anyway! If he's still there, you'll find him at the Hotel Noor, in Chicken Street.'

Chapter 14

'Where've you been?' Mary asked sharply, as they came into the restaurant.

'To a shrine. A saint's tomb, I think,' said Stephen. 'This is Ian.'

Ian sat down and made a close inspection of the menu.

'Are you all right?' asked Mary.

'Just hungry,' said Stephen.

The boy who served in the restaurant came over, smiling.

'Yes, please?' asked the boy.

'I'll have it all,' said Ian.

The boy looked puzzled.

'I want it all, everything on the menu. Some things twice.'

Mary smiled.

'You sound like you haven't eaten for a week.'

'That's how I feel,' said Ian. 'I could eat a horse.'

'If you eat the meat stew, you probably will be eating horse,' said Mary.

Ian looked at Mary and laughed. It was the first time Stephen had seen him laugh, or even smile come to that, and he was struck by a sudden softness in him.

Then Ian ordered up a big meal for all of them.

There was not much to do in the evenings in Herat. What night-life there was took place in the restaurant of the Bamian Hotel. Two German guys – Thomas and

Dieter – played their guitars, and joints circulated freely, though there was no alcohol. A few young Afghanis came in out of curiosity or to practise their English.

The electricity went off as usual, and the waiter brought in oil lamps.

Dieter sang in English, with a light, intense voice and almost over-clear enunciation. Suddenly the restaurant went quiet, and Stephen slumped back and let the words wash over him. It was a Bob Dylan song, 'Mr Tambourine Man'. He had heard it before, but never like this. As he listened he became one with the song, disappearing through the smoke rings of his mind into those weird internal landscapes: the frozen lake and the haunted frightened trees. And then on, beyond, to the other side, to dance beneath the diamond skies...

This was another sort of poetry. Stephen had never heard anything like it before, and it made his spine tingle. But he felt enormously tired. When the song ended, he dragged himself upstairs, lay down on his bed, and fell asleep immediately.

He woke a few hours later in darkness and silence – the window was uncurtained, but the sky was overcast and there were no stars, and no lights on in the whole city. He rolled onto his back and doubled up the hard pillow to raise his head.

'Hi!' said Mary from the bed next to him. 'You awake?'

'Yes,' said Stephen. 'You too?'

'I can't get to sleep,' said Mary. 'I've been lying here for hours, thinking. Stephen, did you get stoned today?'

'I took a puff on a chillum out at the shrine. I didn't think it had much effect, though.'

Mary laughed.

'I never saw anyone as wasted as you two when you walked in this evening! What was the scene there?'

'Some guys in a hut smoking chillums. They were nice. Friendly. A bit sad though. They were talking about taking over the world and making it a better place.'

'You never know. Perhaps they will.'

'Mary... do you ever think about home?'

Mary didn't answer for a long time. Stephen could see nothing, not even an outline of her shape in the bed, and he wondered if she had gone to sleep.

'You know, when I was little, we didn't have a lot,' she said at last. 'It wasn't a great time for me. My dad spent too much on the drink, and my mum was at work, and I had to look after my little sisters when we weren't at school, but what I wanted, what I really, really wanted, was a pet. I thought that was what would make my life all right. I'd have loved a little dog or a kitten, and I'd have looked after it too, but my mum wouldn't let me. So I bought a guinea pig. They couldn't stop me doing that. She was called Cally, and she was so sweet. I took her with me everywhere at first. I took her to school in my pocket, until she weed in my desk and I got caught; after that I had to leave her in a hutch in my bedroom. She didn't like it. I knew she didn't. Who would, locked up on your own all day? At the weekend I took her out to the park, and let her run around between my legs. Then

I lifted my knees, just to see what would happen, just to see where she'd go. She did nothing for a while, just sat there sniffing the air with her nose. And then she ran. She took off, and ran as fast as she could go to some bushes. I can see her now, charging off on her little guinea pig legs! I grabbed at her, but she was too quick.

'I spent the rest of the day looking for her. It was quite wild in the park, and the bushes were thick, with lots of brambles. Sometimes I thought I saw her, but she went further and further into the undergrowth. I didn't really want to catch her, though. She wasn't having much of a life, was she, stuck on her own in my bedroom all day?'

'She wouldn't have survived long though, on her own,' said Stephen.

'Perhaps not. I kept going back though, every day, to try and find her. I gave up in the end. Then, quite a while after – it was autumn, I remember, there were piles of leaves to kick through – I went down to the park just to get out of the house, and there she was, munching away at the grass, looking fat and happy.'

Stephen waited for more, but it didn't come.

'Is that all? Didn't you catch her?'

'No. I just watched her. When I tried to get closer she ran away. I didn't see her again. I expect she died when the frosts came.'

'That's sad.'

'Not really. We're all going to die, aren't we? She was only a guinea pig, anyway.'

There was a flash outside the window, followed by a

171

distant rumble. The nightly thunderstorm was beginning.

'Mary?'

'Yes.'

'Do you think you'll ever go back to Ireland?'

A long rumble of thunder started sharply and faded away slowly, somewhere far off in the hills.

'I might go to Ireland again. The road can take you anywhere. It'd be good to see my sisters for a while. My mum too. But I'm not going back. Not ever. I'm going forward. It's the only way to go.'

A fork of lightning struck the battlements of the citadel, highlighting them brilliantly outside the window, and the crack of thunder followed a second later. In a minute it would rain, and the sound would end all talk and wash them into sleep.

'Ian's a nice guy,' said Mary. 'He's really funny, isn't he? He said he'd like to travel with us when we go to Kabul. We'll get our tickets tomorrow, shall we?'

The next day, after they had bought their tickets, Stephen went to see Jerry. He found him on his own in the garden of the Park Hotel, where Jerry, Reuben and the Green Bus seemed to be the only guests. Jerry was sipping a beer, with a half rolled joint on the table in front of him.

'We're heading for Kabul pretty soon too,' he said. 'We could give you a lift.'

'Thanks, but we've already got our tickets,' said Stephen.

'We'll probably pass each other on the way, then,' said Jerry. 'I hope the Green Bus makes it. She's been feeling the heat a bit. Reuben's a cool guy to have around though, because he knows about engines, and he speaks some of the local language.'

'There's something I wanted to ask you about,' said Stephen. Then he stopped. He knew what he had to say, but when it came to it, it was not so easy.

'Have a beer,' said Jerry. 'God knows where it comes from, but at least it's cold. They've got the only fridge in Herat here.'

'No thanks,' said Stephen quickly. 'Look, Jerry, did you hide a block of hash in my suitcase, back in Istanbul?'

For a moment Jerry was taken aback. He looked down at his beer, and chewed his lower lip. Then he looked up again and met Stephen's eyes.

'I know. It doesn't look good, does it? I really regret doing that, Stephen. It was not the right thing to do, and I know it, even though it actually saved me from twenty years in a Turkish gaol. You've got to believe me though, Stephen, I never thought any harm could come to you from that. Even if the cops had found it, I'd have covered for you – I'd have sworn it was me that put it there. I wouldn't have let you take the rap for that shit, Stephen, no way, I promise you.'

He stopped and sipped his beer. Stephen watched him. It was hard to dislike Jerry really.

Jerry looked at him over his glass, with foam on his moustache and a lop-sided grin.

'What did you do with the stuff when you found it, anyway?'

'I sold it.'

'Hey, good for you, man! Hope you got a good price!'

'Did you know Reuben's thought to be a CIA man?'

Jerry half choked on his beer, then recovered himself.

'Reuben? You're joking.'

'That's what somebody told me in Istanbul.'

'Well that's crap. You shouldn't believe everything you hear, Stephen. Half the time they don't know what they're talking about.'

'And the other half?'

Jerry didn't answer. He looked up at a flock of green parakeets that flew noisily from tree to tree.

'Off to Kabul tomorrow, then . . . I guess you'll find Rob there.'

'Yes,' said Stephen. 'I met a guy who knows him. He even told me the hotel where he's staying.'

'Far out!' said Jerry. He lit his joint and passed it to Stephen, who took a couple of drags and passed it back.

'I'm meeting someone there too,' said Jerry, lounging back in his chair. 'Guess who?'

Stephen shrugged. He couldn't care less who Jerry was meeting.

'Astrid! I just got a telegram. She's flying out and meeting me in Kabul. Maybe we can all get together . . . She'll be surprised to see you here, huh?'

Astrid! Stephen's heart missed a beat. Suddenly the noise of the parakeets was overwhelming. He stood up, noticing little star-shaped fruits forming on the trees.

'I've got to go,' he said. 'I'm meeting Mary.'

'Hey, man, what's the hurry?' said Jerry. 'She'll wait. Stick around and have a beer.'

'See you in Kabul!' said Stephen.

Compared with what they had come through, the journey to Kabul was easy. Most of the way there was a new tarmacked road, with almost no traffic on it, and the bus driver drove steadily, refreshed with regular hits of opium from a large hookah that travelled with him. They stopped for meals in half-ruined caravanserais, and gazed for hours out of the dusty windows of the bus at the shifting shapes and colours of the hills to the north, and the mountain ranges blue in the distance.

They had taken the 'luxury' bus. Stephen was surprised that Mary agreed, as she was usually very careful with her money, but she went along easily with Ian's suggestion. Besides, even the luxury bus was cheap by any Western standards. It was not full, and for much of the time they had four seats between the three of them. Mary sat with Ian, chatting and sharing little joints while Stephen stretched out. It was strange for him at first not to have Mary beside him; he had got so used to her presence on these long bus journeys, but it was good too to have the extra space.

He thought about Rob.

What would Rob think, when he saw him? Would he recognise him? What would he say?

Stephen would stand at his hotel room door, looking cool in his loose shirt and his Afghani hat, and say:

175

'Hi! So I finally found you. Where've you been all this time?'

And Rob would say:

'Stephen! I don't believe it!'

Rob's hair would be quite long and he'd be wearing Afghani clothes, but they would look each other in the eyes, and see the same old Rob, the same old Stephen, and then they'd embrace...

No, that was wrong. They'd never embraced before. At best Rob would stick out a hand and say:

'Hi, bro. Good to see you. I knew you'd catch up with me one day.'

Stephen kept playing it through his head, but somehow his fantasy would not get further than that first meeting. He tried to remember instead.

It was one of Rob's last visits home, and they were standing outside the bike shop in the High Street, putting off going back home. A girl walked by in very high heels and a tight red skirt and a beehive hairdo. Rob followed her with his eye. She knew he was watching, and as she reached the corner she turned back and smiled.

Rob turned to Stephen with a big grin.

'Nice totty! Hey, Stevie, are you interested in girls yet?'

Stephen blushed. He was thirteen. He had just started at public school, and Rob had already left. For the last five years he had been surrounded only by boys, and male teachers. Except for his cousin Harriet.

Harriet was eight months older than him. She was an only child, and they'd played together since he could

176

remember. She had been part of his childhood, and although in the last year her body had changed, just as his had, he had not really taken it in. Then at Christmas, when his family visited her family for tea (only without Rob, who had refused to come), and the adults watched the Queen's speech on their new colour television, Harriet had taken him to her room. Stephen had often been in there. It was decorated with posters of pop singers and horses, with fluffy cuddlies on the bed. She put on a record. She had her own record player, and her parents let her buy all the latest singles. Then they sat on the bed – which was what they always did, and Harriet chattered away to him. Only this time she didn't chat. She pulled him over to her and kissed him.

He had been surprised more than anything at first, but then he started to enjoy it. He was sorry when their parents called them down to tea, and he was looking forward to seeing her again. (In reality, though, by the time he saw her again, she had a boyfriend, and she didn't want to kiss Stephen any more.)

But he didn't mention Harriet to Rob. He just said, 'Yeah, sure. 'Course I am.'

So how could he tell Rob about the Wart? He would, though. He had to tell someone, and Rob was the only one who'd understand.

He would understand, Rob would.

Rob would understand.

★

177

Kabul was very different from Herat – for all the Afghan wildness that enveloped it, it was a proper capital city, with shops and cars and diplomats, and educated women in Western clothes. Exhausted after two days of bus travel, they had collapsed in the dormitory of a cheap hotel near the bus station. The next morning, Stephen woke before the others, asked directions and walked through town to the Hotel Noor. The streets were cool and pleasant in the morning air, and it wasn't far.

He was nervous. After all this time and all this travel, this felt like an ending, a destination. Only it wasn't, of course. At best it was half way, and he still had to get back home somehow. Also there was no certainty it would turn out to be Rob after all. Or even if it was Rob, he might have changed beyond recognition, he might refuse to have anything to do with Stephen.

There was something about the way Ian had talked about him, that made Stephen think he knew more than he was willing to say:

'Rob? I know who he is, but I didn't know him that well. You should have asked Bill – he'd have told you a lot more than I can. You'll find out soon enough, anyway.'

It was true. For better or for worse, he'd find out soon enough, anyway.

The Hotel Noor was in Chicken Street, one of the places where foreign travellers congregated. Foreigners were a lot more numerous here than in Herat, and cafés were springing up to cater for them. One of them had chocolate brownies in the window and a smell of coffee.

Stephen hesitated, tempted. It had been a long time since he had seen – or smelled – anything so Western, and he had had no breakfast. Rob probably wouldn't be up yet, anyway. He went in.

Inside it was cramped and dark, with flies crowded on the ceiling. A couple of Westerners were playing chess, and another was smoking a water pipe. Stephen ordered a coffee and a brownie, and found a seat by the window where he could look out.

It was still too early for the street to be busy. Chickens and dogs went about their business. Three women in full veil went past, chattering loudly. A man carried a huge basket of bright green spinach on his head, and another drove a donkey cart piled high with melons. Two old men sat on their haunches, smoking and talking. A taxi drove past, hooting, and stopped further up the street.

Stephen felt breathless. Perhaps it was the altitude, or perhaps it was his nerves. The brownie was stale, and the coffee was Nescafé, from a tin. It tasted disappointing, and it made him need the toilet. At the back of the café he found the usual stained hole with a dripping tap beside it and an ancient, disgusting can. He was well used to squatting now, and had long since given up using paper.

His stomach felt better, but he was still nervous as he left the café and walked on down Chicken Street. He found the Hotel Noor in a few minutes, but at first he couldn't bring himself to go in, and walked straight on by. Then, taking a deep breath, he turned.

'He isn't there,' he thought to himself. 'I know he isn't

there.' And in some ways, he realised, he wanted him not to be.

This time he turned into the entrance and without pausing went straight up some stairs, at the top of which a young Afghani was sitting behind a desk, reading a book.

He looked up as Stephen approached.

'Hello, you want a room?'

'No,' said Stephen. 'I'm looking for a guy called Rob.'

The man smiled.

'Mr Rob? You want Mr Rob? Can I ask why?'

'I'm his brother,' said Stephen.

'Mr Rob's brother! What is your name?'

'Stephen.'

'Stephen. Wonderful! My name is Yussuf.'

He came out from behind the desk and shook Stephen's hand warmly.

'Your brother has been staying here a long time. I have been teaching him about our great poet Rumi, and he has been teaching me your English literature. William Blake. W.B. Yeats. Wonderful. You like poetry, also?'

'Yes,' said Stephen. 'But, can I see him? Where is he?'

The man's face fell.

'You didn't know? He has just left, five minutes ago. He took a taxi to the bus station, to go to Pakistan. I don't know why. Who wants to go to Pakistan when they can be in Kabul? It is hot like hell down there now. But you can go after him, it's not too late. Go now! I'll fetch you a taxi. Maybe you catch him.'

A taxi! It must have been the one he saw while he had a coffee. Yussuf gripped his arm.

'Go quick! You'll catch him before his bus leaves, for sure.'

The bus station was a big compound of rough ground. Most of the buses were fabulously ornate with chrome or paintwork. Some were hooting for their passengers, some were standing half full, waiting perhaps for their drivers to finish their hookahs, others stood forlornly with smashed windows and flat tyres.

Stephen paid off his taxi, and looked around, trying to figure out which bus, if any, was going to Pakistan. The signs on the front of the buses were written in a script he couldn't read. There were some travel agents' shops near the entrance, but no information point, and probably nobody who spoke English. Near him a crowd was gathered round a bus that was revving its engine. He ran over.

'Pakistan? Pakistan?' he asked.

A man shrugged, then pointed to the other side of the compound.

Stephen ran again.

This bus was magnificent, with swirling paintwork.

'Pakistan?' asked Stephen.

But everyone was caught up with saying goodbye and securing luggage on the roof, too busy to take any notice of a strange Western boy with pink cheeks and an Afghani hat.

Another bus was lumbering over the rough ground. A

man paused from carrying his luggage up to the roof, looked at Stephen briefly, and gestured towards it.

It bumped slowly towards them. It was packed, but more people were still climbing onto it, perching on the luggage on the roof.

'Jalalabad!' someone said beside him, then ran and hung onto the ladder at the back of the bus as it passed.

Stephen looked at the windows, scanning the faces.

And there was Rob.

It was definitely Rob. He had a wispy beard, and long hair tied back with an orange scarf, but it was him all right.

'Rob!' yelled Stephen, running towards the bus. Though with all the noise, Rob couldn't possibly have heard him.

'Rob!' he yelled again, running beside the bus.

Rob turned away and spoke to somebody next to him who Stephen couldn't see. Then he turned back, looked down and saw Stephen. For a second, he looked in Stephen's eyes.

There was a blink of recognition.

Then he looked away.

Stephen stopped. He stood still with the dust billowing around him. The bus turned out of the compound, and disappeared from his sight.

Chapter 15

Stephen walked slowly back to the hotel where he had stayed the night before. It was near the bus station, and easy to find. A few touts approached him, offering hotels or heroin, but he took no notice, and they realised he was preoccupied and left him alone.

So that was it. The end. At least he had seen Rob, though. At least he knew for certain that he was still alive.

Was that it then? Was that what he had come all this way for? Was that what he would tell his mother? 'I went to Afghanistan, and I saw Rob as he left on a bus and he looked at me . . .'

Looked at him – but didn't smile. Didn't shout for the bus to stop, and leap off it and embrace him. Only looked at him. Recognised him. And looked away.

He took a deep breath. He hated Rob, really. He wished he *was* dead. He deserved it . . .

He stopped himself. That wasn't true. He knew he hadn't come here in the end because of Rob, though he wouldn't have come without him. Without him, he would be in school now, getting ready for his O-levels, sweating over logarithms and French grammar, writing essays for the Wart.

He should be grateful. Rob never asked him to come anyway.

He walked slowly on down the dusty street in the hot sun. He felt odd, and it wasn't just because of Rob. He felt a tightness round his stomach and a growing nausea. He regretted the coffee and the brownie.

So here he was. Afghanistan. Somewhere he had hardly heard of before a few weeks ago. He half closed his eyes and let images of green fields, and soft beds, and hot meals, and clean toilets flicker past his eyelids.

How was he going to get home?

He could take an aeroplane. The idea was suddenly very attractive. There was an airport here, after all. Astrid was flying in, so he could fly out. He would phone his parents and ask for the money.

But the thought made him go cold, although the sun was burning hot on his back. Because he had never sent that telegram to his parents. He had meant to many times since Istanbul, but it had never fitted in. They wouldn't know where he was. They'd probably be out of their minds worrying about him by now.

He was as bad as Rob. Worse.

So would he phone them, begging, and run home with his tail between his legs? At least Rob never did that.

And what if they said no?

He was burning hot now, and the glare was hurting his eyes. He must be getting ill. Perhaps he had a touch of sunstroke. Fortunately, it wasn't far to the hotel. Mary would look after him, anyway. She always knew what to do.

He stumbled into the hotel, sat down in the restaurant and ordered some tea. He wondered where Mary was. Perhaps he should go to the dormitory and see if she was awake. He didn't want to stay in the dormitory any longer, though. They'd be better off with a double room. They could go to the Hotel Noor where Rob had been staying. It had seemed like a friendly place.

He sipped his tea; it was strong and sweet and comforting, and he felt a bit better.

Mary came in, with Ian.

'Hi! How's it going?' said Mary.

'I saw Rob,' said Stephen.

'You saw him? That's great! He's still at the Hotel Noor then?'

'No. He just left in the bus. Gone to Pakistan. I saw him through the bus window as he left. That's all.'

Mary sat back for a moment taking it in. Then she leant forward and patted him gently on the knee.

'Don't worry, Stephen. You'll run into him again, further on...'

'That's not the point. I don't want to see him again. He knew I was there. He didn't try to stop the bus or get out. He didn't even smile.'

'It must have been a shock for him as well, seeing you like that,' said Mary.

But she wasn't really listening to Stephen, not the way she usually did. She was full of something else.

'Anyway, we've got a surprise for you too,' she continued.

She turned to Ian and smiled at him. She often smiled, but not like that. It was radiant. Ian took her hand and squeezed it.

'Ian and I...'

Stephen had a powerful sense of *déjà vu*. He knew what was coming, exactly what was coming, the phrasing of the words, the intonation.

'Ian and I want to move into a room together. We want to spend some time on our own. You don't mind, do you, Stephen? It's just . . . well, we really like each other.'

She turned back to Ian and they exchanged that smile again.

Stephen felt hollow. His head was pulsing and his body was painful, though curiously detached.

'Does it actually make any difference whether I mind or not?' he asked.

But Mary and Ian were too busy smiling at each other to hear him.

'Kabul! That's where you get the real shits.' That's what Carl had said to him, back in Teheran. Now Stephen knew what he meant.

He managed to do what had to be done. He moved to the Hotel Noor, and took a single room. It might easily have been the room Rob had just left – he didn't care. He didn't care about Mary either. She could go off with Ian if she wanted. That was her business. He didn't need her. He didn't even tell her where he was going.

He lay down on the bed.

Then he got up from his bed and went to the toilet.

He had hardly shut the toilet door when the cramps gripped him. As he pulled his trousers down, he felt a gush burst from his bum, and at the same time he

186

vomited so powerfully it hit the wall.

Time and place faded out around him. There was no
room for thoughts. He squatted, clutching his knees with
his head down and his eyes shut, as spasm after spasm seized
him, voiding his stomach and his bowels from both ends.

It was a long time before he felt able to open his eyes,
and then he wished he hadn't. The cement walls were
splattered with vomit, and the floor was soiled too. The
toilet was a ceramic pan with a hole in the middle and
raised places to put your feet. It had been relatively clean
before he used it. There was a tap and a tin can as usual,
as well as a small hand-basin and some soap – a real
luxury. He stood up uncertainly, and did his best to clean
up by splashing water around with the tin can. Then he
returned to his room, using the wall for balance.

His trousers were soiled. He took them off and threw
them in a corner, and pulled on his other pair. He was
shaking with cold again, and more exhausted than he had
ever felt. There were two blankets on the bed. He pulled
them over himself and fell fast asleep.

He woke with more stomach cramps, and hurried
back to the toilet, just in time. The pain was just as excru-
ciating, but there was less to come out this time, and he
was soon retching.

Slowly the cramps subsided, leaving a disgusting taste
in his mouth and a curious lightness in his head.

He must drink. He knew that. He would go to the
restaurant and order a tea. He held onto the thought tightly,
and set out down the corridor towards the restaurant.

Every few steps he paused and caught his breath. Lights kept spinning round his head, but at least the cramps had stopped for now.

There was nobody in the restaurant, so he went to the kitchen. Something was cooking – a mutton stew – but the smell revolted him. He asked the boy for tea, and he poured some into a pot from an urn. Stephen sat at a table and drank it; it warmed him and relieved the foul taste. Then he headed back to his room.

He stopped as he passed the toilet and deposited most of the tea he had just drunk in the basin.

He was already shivering again. He made it back to his room, and looked in his bag. He had a plastic water bottle, with some stale but sterilised water in the bottom. He took a tiny sip, just enough to wet his mouth, and put it next to his bed. He got out his bowl too. In an emergency he could vomit into it. Then he pulled the blankets around him again and lay very still with his legs tucked up.

It was better when he lay still. There was a great throbbing in his head, but if he breathed very softly he didn't feel so sick. He lay like that for a long time, and then drifted off to sleep.

When he woke it was dark. There was a light on in the corridor, and he could hear a buzz from the restaurant. He sat up. Immediately he moved, he wanted to vomit again. With a speed that surprised him, he found his way to the toilet, and squatted down. All the blood seemed to have drained from his head, and he was breathing heavily.

The cramps kept coming, so he squatted there for a long time, inhaling the fetid air from the pan, feeling the shivers of nausea running up and down his back, then the moments of relief when a squirt of wind and water exploded out of his bum, and the retching stopped.

At least he didn't make much mess this time.

He returned to his bed, drank a few sips of water, and slept again.

So it went on. Next time, the light was off in the corridor and the restaurant was quiet, though he could hear a guitar playing in a room somewhere. Then it was the middle of the night, dark and silent, and nothing came up at all when he retched, though he managed to shit something. He looked in the pan, and saw globules of mucous and blood.

He wondered if he was going to die.

It wasn't a worrying thought. It made him feel peaceful.

To cease upon the midnight with no pain. That was something he'd read with Mr Wortle. Keats. He died young. *He has awakened from the dream of life.* That was Shelley. He had died young too. At least the pain had gone now, or perhaps it was just that he felt it differently, as if it was occurring in another body, in which he only happened to be visiting. *I is someone else.* Who said that? It was true.

He thought briefly of his mother; she was dim and distant, fading into greyness.

He watched himself stand up and pull up his trousers and wash his hands and open the toilet door and shut it

189

and open the door of his room and go in and shut and lock it behind him and take a sip of water and lie down in the blankets.

He watched himself sleep.

I is someone else.

The cramps woke him in the early morning, as strong as ever. He half slid off the side of his bed, but his legs wouldn't carry him, so he crawled to the toilet.

The door was locked. Someone was using it.

He crawled back to his bed and rested his head on it, clutching his cramping stomach. He picked up his bowl and was sick into it – but it was nothing really, just a bit of acidic phlegm. He couldn't control his bowels any longer, though. In desperation, he crouched down in the corner, squatting over his already soiled trousers.

He lay awake, completely still, watching the light grow brighter outside the window. He could see a tree and a corner of sky. The tree was full of sparrows. The sky was dancing with little white kites, flown from the flat rooftops.

There was a courtyard out there somewhere, where a woman was shouting shrilly at her children, and the children shouted back. A dog barked. A cockerel crowed – far too late.

A large number of flies had taken up residence on the ceiling, and particularly on Stephen's trousers in the corner. When they had nothing better to do they buzzed

190

round his nose. There was a fan hanging from the ceiling. He could have turned it on to dislodge the flies, but he saw no reason to. The flies were entitled to their peace, also.

It was a beautiful place to be. All life was there, and Stephen had no wish ever to go anywhere again.

About mid-morning there was a knock on his door.

With a great effort Stephen managed to call, 'Come in!'

It was Yussuf, the Afghani who had been friends with Rob. He came over to the bed and looked anxiously at Stephen.

'Are you okay?'

'Sort of,' said Stephen. It came out as a hoarse whisper.

'No, you are not okay,' said Yussuf firmly. 'Wait a little. I will find you some help.'

He came back a few minutes later with Thomas, one of the German guys who Stephen had met in the hotel in Herat.

Thomas looked down at Stephen. His eyes were worried.

'How are you doing? You don't look so good.'

'I've got the shits,' whispered Stephen. His voice seemed to have deserted him.

'This man is doctor,' said Yussuf. 'Very clever fellow.'

'I'm not qualified – only studying,' said Thomas, not wanting to give a wrong impression. Stephen didn't care whether Thomas was qualified or not, but he was happy that he was there, that he cared, that he would take charge. He looked up at Thomas' face and saw a great kindness. He looked at Yussuf, and saw the same.

He was a stranger to these people. Why should they care whether he lived or died? But they did. They really did. There was something so wonderful, so extraordinary in that, it brought tears to his eyes. It made him want to live, for them.

Yussuf fetched a glass of hot water from the kitchen, and Thomas mixed something in it.

'Here, drink!'

The smell of it almost overpowered him, but he held back his retching and drank.

It was both sweet and salty, and it relieved the prickly dryness at the back of his mouth. He drank half the glass, and lay back, pleased with his achievement. Then he started to vomit.

Thomas held a bowl in front of him, to catch it.

'Keep drinking, man. Don't worry if it comes back up. Just keep drinking. And lie here quiet. I come back in an hour.'

Stephen did as he was told. Whatever medicine Thomas gave him seemed to work, and he soon felt a little better. His cramps were lighter, so that he could endure them till they passed and no longer needed to visit the toilet.

He lay on his bed dozing and listening to the sounds outside his window. It was hot in the afternoon, and Thomas put on the fan for him and woke up the flies.

Time passed in little trickles.

Stephen began to wonder about his trousers.

They lay where he had thrown them, where he had

squatted on them. He could see them from his bed, looking as if they were covered in currants, which he knew to be flies. Neither Yussuf nor Thomas had noticed them, or perhaps they were just too disgusting to mention.

The light faded. Thomas brought him some hot lemon, and sat on his bed while he sipped it.

'You have dysentery,' he said. 'It might be cholera, but I don't think so. The dysentery is really bad in Kabul. But you'll get better, as long as you keep drinking. Also, I will give you some pills.'

After he had gone, Stephen eased himself out of bed, pleased to find he could stand again, and went to inspect his trousers. The flies rose up as he reached them. He looked, but although they were dirty, they were not covered in blood and shit as he thought. There were just some brown marks. He picked them up and sniffed them. They smelled bad, but not that bad. How was it possible?

The flies! The flies ate the shit, obviously... And where did the flies go next? To people's faces, to the meat hanging in the street, to the cakes in the cafés.

He dropped his trousers back in the corner and returned to bed.

Two days later he felt well enough to sit with Thomas and his friend Dieter in the restaurant and eat a small omelette. Well enough to talk to Yussuf about English poetry. Yussuf was not in fact the manager. He was a student from Kabul university who did shifts at the hotel, partly to earn some money, but mainly to improve his already near perfect English. He talked to everyone.

'Sorry you didn't catch your brother,' he said to Stephen. 'He is an interesting fellow.'

Yussuf could have told him much more. Stephen knew that. But he didn't want to hear it.

'Yeah, well, he's got his life and I've got mine,' he blocked. Yussuf nodded and smiled, understanding.

Stephen didn't stay long in the restaurant though. The cramps and nausea had finished, but he was simply exhausted. For most of the day he lay on his bed, watching the fan turn, and attending to the sounds and smells that came through the open window with the flies.

He was alone again. Mary was with Ian somewhere. She didn't even know he was ill, and it was better that way. Because in reality he had always been alone. At home, at school – always there was a bubble around him, out of which he looked, which others peeped in through occasionally. If he had gone to Thierry's he would have been alone too, more so than here, where the chatter of children, the birdsong, the call of the muezzin at prayer time, and the smells of dust and spices and rancid hay went through him and became part of him.

He thought back. Was there a time before, when his parents had not been partly strangers?

How young could he remember?

He remembered a picnic – a hillside and a stream, and bracken towering over him, so high he could disappear. He pushed the stalks apart, and stepped into the forest of ferns, and instantly he had disappeared. There were little plants that grew in there, and insects. He pushed on through – the tops of the bracken were over his head, and hardly stirred as he moved. A lark was singing.

He sat down.

'Nobody will ever find me here,' he thought.

Time passed. He didn't know how long, but after a while he could hear them looking for him. He didn't move. He knew if he kept very still, he was invisible.

Rob was rushing around shouting excitedly. His mother was calling his name, with an edge of desperation. From a few feet away from him, his father said: 'He was here a minute ago. He can't have gone far.'

And then Stephen stood up, pushed the bracken aside with his arms and said joyfully: 'Here I am!' And his mother rushed over and whisked him into her arms, and clutched him to her, and he was surprised, because there was anger in her voice and tears in her eyes.

'Never do that again!' she said, catching her breath. 'Never, ever, ever!'

The fan turned. Day became night, and night became day. He ate more, and felt a little strength return. He took his dirty trousers into the shower and rubbed in washing soap and pounded them, as Mary had taught him to do. He washed his shirt too. Then, almost as an afterthought, he washed his body.

He smiled as he looked down at himself. He was stick thin. How his mother would disapprove! But he liked it.

195

Apart from his pink skin, he was the same as everyone else here.

He returned to his bed. It was safe. Despite Thomas's pills he was not ready yet to go back out alone into Afghanistan, and on into the future that awaited him.

But he would be soon.

Chapter 16

'Don't you feel like some good food?' asked Thomas. 'Come with us. We are going to the Khyber Restaurant.'

To Stephen's eyes, the Khyber Restaurant was grand – a plate glass and concrete building with flags hanging outside and liveried attendants. Inside, it was a Western style cafeteria with a long stainless steel counter and formica topped tables. It was not expensive, and it was full of Westerners – diplomats, businessmen, and some 'real' tourists, as well as many faces he had already seen on his travels.

Martin was there, with his long red hair. And Carl and Andreas.

On a whim, Stephen went over to Martin's table and greeted him.

'Hi!' said Martin. 'You got here!'

'Just about,' said Stephen. 'By the way, you remember that dollar I lent you . . . ?"

'Yeah sure,' said Martin, reaching in an inner pocket of his waistcoat and pulling out a roll of bills. 'Thanks, man. You really saved me a lot of hassle there.'

He grinned at Stephen, showing his bad teeth.

It was the first time Stephen had left his hotel since his illness, and it seemed at first like an overwhelming opulence. There were all kinds of Western foods on display – hamburgers, hot dogs, pizzas, espresso coffee, apple pie. But since he had been ill he was wary of Western food. He took a plate of rice and meatballs and sat down with Thomas and Dieter.

They were talking about visas. They were leaving for India in a few days, going through Pakistan, and needed the right documents. And it was going to be hot.

Although they were both German, they talked in English so that Stephen could understand. It was nice of them, but he wasn't all that interested. The future was another country. He was here.

And then he saw Astrid. She was at the other end of the restaurant and she had her back to him, but he recognised her instantly from the curve of her neck. She was sitting at a table alone.

'Excuse me,' he said to Thomas and Dieter. 'I just saw an old friend. I have to go and talk to her.'

He stood up, and walked over to her table.

'Hello!'

She looked up, and smiled.

Then she smiled some more. Her smile spread wide across her face. It was as if she couldn't stop it.

'Stevie!'

She was about to jump up and hug him, but then she remembered she was in Afghanistan, and just squeezed his hand.

He sat down.

'Hi! Jerry told me you were here. We've been looking out for you. Where have you been hiding?'

'I've been ill,' said Stephen. 'I had dysentery, I think.

This is the first time I've left the hotel since I got here, practically.'

He couldn't stop smiling either. She looked more beautiful than ever. She was wearing a white embroidered dress and a little waistcoat, and a muslin scarf threaded with silver.

'You look thin. But good!' she said.

She kept looking at him. She hadn't let go of his hand. He gave hers a little squeeze and pulled his away.

'Where's Jerry?'

She made a face.

'He had to go. Business. You know Jerry, he always has to go somewhere. He went up in the mountains with Reuben.'

'Scoring hash?'

She laughed.

'You learn quick, don't you, Stevie?'

'He left you here on your own?'

'Just a couple of days. He knows I don't like the business. It freaks me out. But I love Afghanistan! It is wonderful, huh?'

'I liked Herat,' said Stephen. 'I haven't had much time to see Kabul, yet.'

'What about your girlfriend?' asked Astrid.

'Girlfriend?'

'Jerry said you had a girlfriend. You were travelling together.'

'Oh, you mean Mary...' He wondered how much to say. Did Jerry think they had been sleeping together? 'We weren't really together, like that. Anyway she left me. Just before I got ill. Went off with a bloke called Ian. I don't know where she is now.'

'Poor you...'

'Not really,' he said.

They left the restaurant together. Dieter and Thomas stared at them wide-eyed as he briefly introduced Astrid, and he could feel the heads turning as they walked out.

'We go to my place,' she said, and led him to a taxi.

They drove slowly round the square. There was a marvellous fountain playing in the middle, and the roof of a palace sparkled in the sun on one side, while on the other a half-finished concrete office block was squatted by vegetable stalls and street food sellers in an impromptu market.

Astrid smiled at him. He sat back and let himself be driven, feeling peaceful and happy. She was the most beautiful girl in the world, and he was with her. And Jerry was miles away, stoned out of his head probably, in an Afghan village.

The taxi took them to the northern suburbs, the wealthiest part of the city, with villas hidden among the trees, protected by guard dogs and high walls. It was like being back in Europe... if it hadn't been for the brown mass of the hills rising upon every side, and the extraordinary quality of the light. Stephen noticed a British Council library. It would be good to spend a day there among books and English voices.

They drew into the sweep of Astrid's hotel. The taxi driver expected a big tip, and got it.

Stepping out of the taxi, Stephen suddenly felt dirty. It was true that Astrid dressed like a hippy, but she did it with style and expense. She could have gone anywhere. Whereas he... He looked down anxiously at his baggy Afghan trousers to see if they were stained.

Astrid saw his hesitation.

'Don't worry. You look fine. Anyway, you can look how you like here.' She led him into the lobby, where a man in a suit behind the reception desk handed her her keys.

'Can you send up some tea and things?' she asked vaguely.

They went up the marble staircase to the first floor. Astrid opened a door and ushered Stephen in.

'Nice, huh?'

It was. The floor was carpeted with thick-piled tribal rugs and the walls were hung with tapestries; the bed was set apart in an alcove, and big cushions were set around a low, carved wooden table. French windows opened onto a balcony with a view of a giant mulberry tree.

There was a scent of musk, mingled with roses.

Astrid dropped onto a cushion. Stephen sat down opposite her. The opulence made him self-conscious. He felt an itch round his midriff – a flea probably – and longed to scratch it, but he didn't dare.

Astrid smiled at him and flicked back her hair.

'So,' she said. 'What have you been doing all this time, Stevie?'

For a moment Stephen couldn't think of anything to say. How could this Princess relate to the bruising bus journeys, the junkie hotels, the little satisfactions of finding a bottle of milk or a tin of Quaker oats in a shop, the sweetness of the fruit, the frightfulness of the toilets? Then he remembered the time he had been chased in Iran, and the family who had rescued him. That was a story he could tell.

Astrid listened, wide-eyed.

'You make me feel so boring,' she said. 'You have so much adventure, Stevie.'

There was something about the way she said his name that gave him a tingle up and down his spine.

The tea came, with china bowls of cashew nuts and sultanas.

'And you?' asked Stephen. 'Where have you been?'

'I went home, to Germany. It was boring. But I am frightened sometimes of what Jerry does. So when the danger is too great, I run away. But then I come back. I always come back.'

She sighed, and then she smiled again, looking straight into his eyes.

'I am so happy to see you, looking so good. I was really worried about you after I left Istanbul. That you would be all right. But you're tough really, aren't you?'

Stephen shrugged. He didn't feel tough. He had gone along with Jerry and then he had gone along with Mary, that was all. But he didn't want to contradict her.

'I remember Rob,' she said. 'When I see your eyes I

202

think of his. So blue! What a crazy guy! We lived in the same place, on an island in Spain.'

She paused. She was ready to say more, but Stephen looked away, out of the window where some parakeets were squawking among the ripe mulberries. He didn't want to hear about Rob.

She took a small enamel box out of her bag, and a packet of cigarettes.

'Shall we smoke a little joint? You do smoke now, don't you? I remember in the Green Bus you didn't – it was so cute – but everybody smokes in Afghanistan. It's different like that here. Another reality, where our dreams come true.'

She took out a lump of hash, and crumbled some in her palm.

Stephen watched her. Suddenly he did want to know about Rob after all – his brother, who was like a stranger now. What did Astrid know about him? How had she known him?

'Rob – what was he like, when you . . . were with him?'

'Rob? Yeah, crazy. He looks like you, but he isn't really, is he? He is hard where you are soft. Still, he's a great guy. He was taking a lot of acid – LSD, you know? – and he was singing in a rock band with some American guys. He sang like nobody else. He wrote songs too. Weird songs, but we loved them. Did you ever find him?'

'He was here in Kabul. But he's gone. I just missed him.'

'Pity for you,' said Astrid.

'I don't care really,' said Stephen. 'I'm not here for him. I'm here for me.'

They smoked. They looked in each other's eyes. Astrid's eyes were pools, her smile was a gate to a forbidden land.

That itch again.

'Astrid . . . Do you think I could take a bath?'

'Oh yes! You'll love the bathroom!'

She offered her hand to help him up, and he brushed against her, catching her fragrance. He wanted to hold her to him, but it wasn't the time. He felt too dirty.

She led him to the bathroom.

It was beautiful, with patterned green and blue tiles, scented soap, a basin where hot and cold water bubbled in little fountains, a shower in the middle of the ceiling.

He threw his clothes into the corner and immersed himself in the shower, soaping himself all over, then shutting his eyes and letting the hot water foam around him, washing away his dirt, his illness, his thoughts.

He opened his eyes, and there was Astrid. She was watching him, a bottle of oil in one hand. She was naked.

She stepped forward, smiling, so that the water from the shower splashed down the front of her face, her breasts, her stomach.

Stephen leant forward and kissed her. It seemed the most natural thing in the world.

'I brought some oil,' she said between kisses. 'I thought maybe you would like a little massage.'

He lay on a tiled platform and she rubbed the scented

oil all over his body. In the garden, someone was playing a flute in the Afghani style, with trills like birdsong.

She kissed the small of his back, very gently, just the brush of her lips. Then she turned him over. He kept his eyes shut. He was afraid to look, in case it was too much, or in case it all disintegrated, or he died from too much pleasure. He slipped his mind in neutral, and the insides of his eyelids danced with coloured lights.

She lay down next to him.

'Stevie . . . !' she whispered.

He turned towards her, still with his eyes closed, and his mouth found hers.

'Stevie,' she whispered again, after a long while. 'Is it your . . . first time?'

Stephen opened his eyes. Astrid lay next to him, and her naked form was more beautiful even than he imagined. But she was a girl. Only a girl. Not a princess, nor a goddess.

'Yes,' he whispered. Then froze with the lie, and the memory it brought back.

'What's the matter?'

'I don't know . . .'

Should he tell her?

And spoil this perfect moment.

But it was already spoiled.

Astrid moved her body a fraction away from his, and looked at him, searching his eyes with hers. She stroked his nose with her finger.

'I want you so much, Stevie. I don't know why. You are

just so beautiful. So... innocent. I never wanted anyone more.'

'I know,' he said. 'Me too.' But he was already gulping back pain.

'We shouldn't fall in love, Stevie. We shouldn't do that. Because I'll go back to Jerry. I always do.'

'Yes,' he said. 'You are right. I have to go.'

Because he couldn't tell her. He couldn't.

But she threw her arms around his neck and they kissed, and they held each other, tight and naked, lying on the marble slab.

As usual a line of poetry came into his head. One the Wart had taught him. He wished it wouldn't – it just got in the way.

So, so break off this last lamenting kiss
Which sucks two souls, and vapours both away.

He pulled from the embrace, almost roughly, dried himself quickly, and pulled on his dirty clothes. He wanted to go, just walk out of the room without looking back.

But he did turn.

Astrid was sitting up – was she wet from the shower, or were those tears on her cheeks? She tried to smile.

'It's my fault. I wish you'd stay... we could talk.'

'No,' said Stephen. 'It's my fault... I'm not ready...'

'I know.'

He stood for a long moment, held by the beauty of her eyes.

'Thank you,' he said. 'I love you, Astrid.'

'I love you too, Stevie.'

Then, not even knowing what drove him, what madness kept him from her, he tore himself away.

Turn thou ghost that way, and let me turn this.

Through the bedroom. Down the stairs. Past the reception desk.

And let ourselves benight our happiest day.

Stephen walked. He didn't know what he was doing, he just walked. He didn't know what he had just done, or why, only that he had to walk, and keep walking until the shame and the rage and the passion that were in him had driven him to the end of wherever he was going.

He walked. The posh suburbs gave way to mud dwellings, where the children crowded round him. He hardly noticed them. He crossed a road, and saw a track leading to the hills, and followed it.

He walked. It was mid-afternoon. The heat was terrible and no birds sang. He had no water with him, nothing but his little bag with passport and money, that rubbed his chest where Astrid had rubbed him with oil and kissed him, such a short time ago.

He walked, climbing between fields of barley. He sat down to catch his breath under some poplar trees by a farm, where the whole family came out to marvel at him. A boy came up shyly and offered him a slice of water melon, and he ate it greedily, letting the juice dribble down his chin. Below him, the city of Kabul stretched across the valley.

He walked, up among rocks and thorns, where goats

stared at him square-eyed, and a hawk hovered, looking for mice.

He walked, as the air cooled and the light softened, and his thoughts softened too. At last, he found himself on a ridge, the pass to the next valley. Beyond, wave upon wave of mountains led through layers of shadows to snow-capped peaks. A world vast, empty, desolate, beyond imagination.

He sat on a rock, facing East. He put his head in his hands and felt the setting sun warm his back.

And remembered.

Chapter 17

April might be the cruellest month, but February was the worst at Grindlesham. Spring term meant Rugby, which Stephen hated. Soames was captain of the House Rugby team, and Stephen was made to play because he was undoubtedly strong, and it was 'good for him'. He stood around most of the time with wet feet and numb toes, getting chilblains while Soames with a contorted face yelled at him to 'pull a finger out'.

Out of what?

Afterwards there were stinking bodies in the shower, and copies of *Titbits* circulated surreptitiously. Dark came early, and the heat pipes rattled in his cubicle, without warming him much.

Before Christmas he had gone out with Mr Wortle in his car, looking at churches. It had been fun. Away from the college, Mr Wortle was relaxed, erudite, amusing.

'Call me Charles,' he said. 'It's my real name. I always think one never quite gets used to identifying with one's surname. You don't mind if I call you Stephen, do you?'

Stephen found it impossible to call him Charles, so he avoided calling him anything, but he grew more familiar, teasing him about the way he let his hair grow over his collar.

'Oh, you young people, you're so conservative,' rejoined Mr Wortle. 'But don't worry, you'll have yours down to your shoulders soon, like they do in California. I should like to live in California. All that sunshine. All that youthful energy.'

'Why do you teach at Grindlesham, then?' asked Stephen.

'Why? Oh, why indeed? I'm not much good for anything else you know. Besides...' He smiled sweetly. '...I like boys!'

'I don't know what I'll do when I grow up,' said Stephen, pensively. His lack of ambition to do or become anything had been worrying him lately.

'When you grow up? Ah, perish the thought! Don't even think of it. Stay young forever!'

But after Christmas the weekend trips stopped. Stephen missed them. They had been a ray of sunshine in his drab existence. Mr Wortle became more distant again, and though he was full of praise for Stephen's school work, Stephen was never alone with him. Instead, he took to hanging out in the art room with Strychnine. You could make your own cups of tea there, and it was warm and nobody bothered you.

'What about the Wart, then?' asked Strychnine as he glued yoghurt pots over fairy lights on a large piece of hardboard.

'What about him?'

'He's got a crush on you, hasn't he?'

'What do you mean?'

'Of course he has. The way he looks at you!'

'I don't see him much any more. I think he avoids me.'

'That's why, then. He's embarrassed about it. Do you fancy him?'

Stephen was shocked for a moment.

'Don't be stupid! I like him though. He's all right.'

Strychnine switched on the fairy lights to see the effect, then squeezed out some oil paint and put little squiggles onto the pots.

'I read a book in the library. Some of those books, I don't know how they get in there. It was about that French poet, Rimbaud, the one the Wart goes on about sometimes. He was only fifteen, same age as us. And he went off with this old bald poet called Verlaine and they lived in London and got completely drunk all the time and buggered each other stupid. Would you believe it? And then they give us their poems to read!'

He finished the squiggles, and jiggled the paintbrush in some turpentine, grinning at Stephen through his crooked teeth.

'I bet they had good fun though!'

Stephen trudged to tea along the colonnade, while a sleety rain slanted across the quadrangle. It was a particularly nasty evening. He had a cold starting in the roof of his mouth, which had got a lot worse for playing Rugby in thick mud and sepulchral gloom.

The food was uneatable, as usual, and he had to sit next to Soames. They had lost at Rugby, and Soames was not in a good mood.

'You were pathetic today, Wiston,' he commented

between mouthfuls of nameless sludge. 'What did you think you were supposed to be doing – picking daisies?'

'That's what we do in the summer, Soames, when we play cricket.'

'What *you* do. Why didn't you stop that guy scoring a try? You were right in front of him. You could easily have tackled him. It was pathetic.'

'No. *You're* pathetic, and the game's pathetic. I'm not pathetic. I just want to keep my front teeth.'

At least there was a meeting of the Aesthetes to look forward to that evening.

Mr Wortle's room felt like heaven – the soft lights, the wood fire, the leather sofas and the smell of cigar smoke. Mr Wortle himself sat on a hard chair at the end of the room with his legs crossed and a gentle smile, while the boys lounged on the sofas sipping beer and discussing Oscar Wilde. They read a scene from *The Importance of Being Earnest*, then some stanzas from 'The Ballad of Reading Gaol':

> *Yet each man kills the thing he loves,*
> *By each let this be heard,*
> *Some do it with a bitter look,*
> *Some with a flattering word,*
> *The coward does it with a kiss,*
> *The brave man with a sword!*

'You can't doubt the authenticity of Oscar's anguish,' remarked Mr Wortle. 'I think he always knew, though,

212

that his work would live. There was nobody more shamed and vilified in his lifetime, yet his plays are still performed, his poems are still read, his children's stories are re-issued and re-issued, while most of his contemporaries . . . gone and forgotten! Because they didn't have the heart, and they didn't have the wit.'

'Why was he sent to prison?' asked Stephen naively.

There was a hush. Some of the older boys knew, but they all looked to Mr Wortle. He had taken out a small cigar, and was rolling it between his fingers.

'For falling in love,' he said finally, looking straight at Stephen with his big, deep eyes. 'The love that dare not speak its name. His beloved Bosey, the son of the Marquess of Queensberry, a beautiful boy, who betrayed him of course. There was a court case. Oscar lost. And that was that, really. Prison, disgrace, exile and an early death. Do times change, do you think? Would anyone be more accepting now?'

After the meeting finished, Stephen lingered at the door, last to leave and reluctant to go out into the cold of the night.

'If you've got a moment, Stephen, come back in,' said Mr Wortle.

He was standing in front of his fireplace, warming the back of his trousers. He had lit his cigar.

He smiled at Stephen, almost shyly.

'Did you enjoy the discussion tonight?'

'Yes. Well, I always do.'

'*The Importance of Being Earnest* is on in Oxford next month. We should organise a group to go and see it.'

'I'd enjoy that,' said Stephen.

Mr Wortle pulled at his cigar and let the smoke out slowly. He looked at Stephen and then he looked away.

'I wonder...' he said, and stopped.

'Yes?' prompted Stephen.

'I've been missing our weekend jaunts. Have you?'

'Oh yes! Yes, I miss them a lot.'

'Let's go out again then, on Saturday. I know! We could go over to Stratford. It's not that far, and it will be useful research for your O-levels. Then we'll have supper at a Berni or something on the way back.'

'Thanks,' said Stephen. 'I'd like that.'

Mr Wortle tapped the side of his nose.

'Don't tell anyone. Just our little secret, eh?'

'I'll have to get Mr Husting's permission.'

'Yes of course. That won't be a problem, I'm sure. I'll have a word with him myself.'

The weather turned colder. It froze on Friday night, and Saturday dawned grey and foreboding. Stephen's cold was worse.

At least he wouldn't have to play Rugby though. He was going to Stratford with the Wart! Mr Husting had signed the leave form for the day with a sardonic comment:

'I suppose you might as well get some culture then, Wiston. I can see we're never going to do anything with you at sport.'

After lessons, Stephen slipped off as quietly as possible, but Soames saw him leaving through the back gate.

'Off with your pervy friend, are you?' he shouted after him.

Stephen took no notice. He just wanted to be away from the school. He wanted to be sitting in Mr Wortle's car, the heater on and the window slightly open, driving fast along motorways or slowly along country lanes, with Mr Wortle holding forth in his gentle voice on poetry, or art, or tolerance and social change.

It was a long drive to Stratford. Mr Wortle put on his car radio and they listened to Beethoven on the Third Programme. Stephen sank back in his seat and let the music wash over him.

A few flakes of snow fell against the windscreen. It was amusing to watch them settle, and the wipers almost immediately whisk them away. A thin skin of snow was forming along the verges.

It wasn't the best of visits. Stratford was empty and bitterly cold. They traipsed round Ann Hathaway's cottage, which was dull, then they had tea in the café of the Swan Theatre, among blown-up photographs of old theatre productions. Stephen would have loved to watch a performance, but it was off season and there was only a ballet, which had already started. Besides, they didn't have time.

Mr Wortle looked nervously at his watch. It was growing dark already, and the snow was falling more thickly.

'I think we'd better be getting back, actually,' he said. 'We'll stop for supper the other end. The roads may be getting tricky.'

Outside, it had become suddenly beautiful. They stepped through the dusk in crisp snow, and all around them the trees and the buildings had turned white. The streetlamps came on, and each one illuminated its own orange pool of dancing snowflakes. Some children, in gloves and scarves, were already playing snowballs.

Stephen looked round at Mr Wortle, who at once turned and caught his eye. They shared a smile.

'Escape to Faerieland!' said Mr Wortle. 'For both of us, eh?'

Stephen nodded. It was easy to forget, in Grindlesham, the whole world going on out here in all its beauty.

They didn't talk much on the way back. It was difficult driving and Mr Wortle had to concentrate, peering through a thickening blizzard, following the fast extinguishing tracks of other cars on a white road.

He was a good driver, though, Mr Wortle. Stephen felt safe.

There was still a long way to go and it wasn't getting any better. For a while the road was gritted, and slushy, but little traffic came the other way and none overtook them. Then the gritting ended and they were driving on an inch of snow.

The headlamps picked out a car that had gone off the road. Mr Wortle stopped, and he and Stephen got out and helped push it back straight again. The driver thanked them and they went on in convoy to the next village.

The exertion of pushing the car left Stephen feeling exhilarated, but also hungry. They'd only had sandwiches for lunch and a quick tea at the theatre. His nose was running. He dabbed at it with a handkerchief. He was beginning to wonder when or if they would get back, going at this pace. The blizzard was stronger than ever.

As if reading his thoughts, Mr Wortle took his eyes off the road for a moment and glanced at him.

'I'm not sure we're going to make it back tonight. But there's a little hotel I know, just past here, where we could get a meal and stay the night. I'll ring College, so they're in the picture. Then we can go on in the morning after the snow ploughs have been through. What do you say?'

'Sounds great,' said Stephen.

It was an old place, with low ceilings and black beams, and a huge inglenook chimney with a fire. It was good to get into the warmth and light, and hear the sounds of merriment from the bar, and smell the food cooking in the kitchen.

Stephen sat in the lobby, while Mr Wortle went to the desk to ask about rooms. After a few minutes, he came back, with a look of concern.

'I'm afraid they don't have any singles. They only have one double left. What do you think? Would you mind sharing?'

Stephen grinned.

'As long as you're not worried about catching my cold!'

217

Mr Wortle smiled back at him. It was a very nice smile. Very friendly. Very warm.

'I'll take a chance on that one. It will be better than a snowdrift, anyway!'

Mr Wortle had a suitcase in the back of his car, with overnight essentials – even including a spare toothbrush. Stephen was surprised at his forethought.

'Just a precaution, dear boy. I always take it in the car. Just in case. Anyway, let's have a spot of dinner before anything else. I'm sure you're famished. I am.'

The food was good – compared with college food, it was wonderful. There were candles on the tables, a soft light, music in the background and a hum of chat from the other diners. Eating made Stephen's cold feel better.

'Rather fortunate in a way,' said Mr Wortle. 'I'd certainly much rather be here than at College. Wouldn't you?'

'Oh yes,' said Stephen.

'Especially in your company,' added Mr Wortle, meeting Stephen's eyes.

Stephen automatically looked away, and then he looked back. Mr Wortle was still looking at him with that shy, inviting smile that he had. Like a Cheshire Cat, Stephen thought. A Cheshire Cat. He hadn't drunk any alcohol, but he was sleepy and half intoxicated from the snow, and his cold, and the warmth of the dining room. It was unaccustomed...

'I have to say, of all the pupils I have been privileged to teach, Stephen, you have the most developed sensibilities... Did you enjoy our discussion about Oscar Wilde?'

'*Yet each man kills the thing he loves . . .*' quoted Stephen, pleased with his memory.

Mr Wortle looked down at his hands.

'Oscar had a lovely wife, sons that he adored, a huge reputation, and he risked it all for his love for a spoilt, precocious boy. He risked and lost. What do you think? Was that noble? Or was it . . . criminal?'

Something like a cold draught went up Stephen's spine. He put down his knife and fork. All his sleepiness had gone. He looked across at Mr Wortle, who was looking at his plate and poking his salad with a fork. He noticed the curve of Mr Wortle's nose, the flecks of grey in his hair, the purple of his chin where he shaved.

'You're talking about yourself, Sir, aren't you?'

'Please don't call me Sir. I've told you. Call me Charles.'

Mr Wortle looked up and met his eyes again. Stephen wanted to look away, but he couldn't. Those eyes were too big, too kind. The chill that ran up and down his spine had a thrill to it too.

Mr Wortle reached out and touched his hand.

'You're a very special boy, Stephen. You know that.'

He had enjoyed it. That was the point. He had enjoyed it.

Mr Wortle ordered a bottle of wine with his meal, but hardly drank any. He had what was left brought up to the room, and invited Stephen to drink it with him, until he felt light and giggly. Then, gently, slowly, delicately, he took Stephen in his arms.

The smell of him. It came back to Stephen, sitting

219

on the Afghan mountainside. The exact smell of sweat and cologne, exciting and repelling him even in the memory.

And then Mr Wortle kissed him. He kissed him on the forehead and the eyes, and then on the lips, but Stephen moved his head away.

'I've got a cold,' he mumbled, and Mr Wortle – 'Charles' – accepted the excuse. Instead, he undid Stephen's trousers, and gently stroked his groin.

Stephen could remember it exactly, that feeling: a huge erection, huge excitement, the excitement of the forbidden – and a huge revulsion, that only made the excitement greater.

'Charles' took Stephen's hand and put it on his own genitals.

Stephen shut his eyes. It was easier that way. He concentrated on the colours dancing on the inside of his eyelids. His body was dissolving and he felt like soft wax.

'Charles' pulled him down onto the bed. They were both naked, their clothes mixed together in an untidy heap on the floor. He rolled Stephen onto his front, and lay on top of him, caressing him, kissing his hair and stroking his neck...stroking his neck...stroking his neck. In his hand he held a pot of vaseline.

'Stephen,' he whispered. 'You are so beautiful, Stephen. You have no idea how beautiful you are... You'll enjoy this, Stephen, I know you will...'

Afterwards, lying on his own with a bruised bum among

soiled sheets, he could hear the Wart snoring in the twin bed next to his.

He *had* enjoyed it, in a way. That was the worst of it. A weird pleasure, an overwhelming excitement that was only increased by his sense of shame. And there was no one he could tell about it. Ever. Not his friends, nor his mother, nor his father. There was no one to help him make sense of it. Except for Rob.

And Rob had gone.

The sun was setting over a distant ridge. The sky was a bruise of colour. The world was vast, far bigger than anyone could ever imagine. Vast with potentials, vast with desires, vast with longings, vast with sorrow.

Stephen thought of Astrid, with a twist of longing. Her naked body. He wanted her more than ever, but it would never be now.

She said she loved him. What did that mean? Was it anything more than words?

Did Mr Wortle love him?

No. Whatever Mr Wortle had felt, it had not been love. He was not capable of it. When you love someone, you don't want to hurt them.

Yet each man kills the thing he loves . . .

Surely that couldn't be true.

He stood up, ready to walk back down. It would take some hours, but there was a moon to light him.

From somewhere, inexplicably in that wilderness, came a smell of flowers.

The last rays of the sun went out, and a cool wind blew through a shadowy world, with distant snow peaks shining brilliant gold. As Stephen walked, the past and the future fell away from him. There was only this moment. The present. Now.

Part 4:
The Drunken Boat

...to reach the unknown by the derangement of all the senses
                                              Arthur Rimbaud

Chapter 18

Stephen stood in the river Ganges, wearing nothing but a loin-cloth. The water tumbled around his legs, splashing his waist. It was freezing cold – snow-melt from the Himalayas – but he didn't mind. He enjoyed the contrast with the burning heat of the mid-day sun on his back.

Nobody was watching, but he looked good and he knew it. His hair had grown and hung golden on his shoulders, bleached by the sun. His face had grown thin to match his body, but he was strong and fit, and his eyes had a new intensity.

He needed nothing. He belonged to nobody but himself.

In his hands he held the bag that he kept round his neck, with his passport, money and documents. He had already given away the last of the dollar bills he got for the hash in Istanbul. Now he took out his passport, and opened it. A photo of himself in a suit smiled out at him, chubby-faced and innocent. He smiled back at it, then carefully tore it out and dropped it in the current.

'*Om Nama Shivaya,*' he intoned, as he watched it float away.

He went through the pages one by one, looking at the stamps that showed the progress of his journey, taking his time to remember each bit as it happened . . . the arrival in Calais . . . Greece . . . Turkey . . . extravagant whole page visas for Iran and Afghanistan in mostly Arabic script with odd words of English: '*Single journey via Islam Quala*' ... finally Pakistan ... India. When he was ready with each page he pulled it out and watched it float down the Ganges till it vanished from sight, his past floating away from him.

He held up the blue embossed cover with its lion and unicorn, and the pompous message from 'Her Britannic Majesty's Principal Secretary of State'. Empty nonsense. Remembering with amused embarrassment how he had once believed in all that, he tore the cover in half and threw the two pieces as far as he could. They disappeared into the turbulence in mid-stream.

He pulled out two scruffy bits of paper, vaccination certificates for typhoid and cholera that he had got in Istanbul with Mary, at serious risk of catching hepatitis from the needles. You couldn't cross a border without them. But he would be crossing no more borders. He made them into paper boats and watched them sail away.

All that was left in his bag now was a tattered black and white photograph of two ageing people in an English garden. It was the last thing he had that he had brought with him from England, this photo of his parents. He had hardly looked at it in all this time, but somehow it had stayed with him.

He looked at it now.

His father, not quite meeting the camera's eye, trying to smile.

His mother with the face of determined cheerfulness

that she sometimes put on for visitors, but her eyes heavy with sadness.

Trees and flowers. The garden wall that he knew so well . . .

He was not going back now. It was too late. Besides, they wouldn't want him. They'd hardly even recognise him.

He had sent that telegram, finally, from Lahore. He was glad about that – they would know where he was, that he was all right, and Rob too. That was enough.

He took a last look, and then tore the photo into the tiniest pieces he could and scattered them on the water like petals. The bag had no further use, so he dropped it, and an eddy sucked it under.

It was done. Finished. No more past. Only the present, unfolding itself in an endless succession of moments.

He walked further out into the river, took a deep breath and immersed himself in the freezing water. He felt its roar around him – the roar of eternity. He lost his foothold and was carried away by the current, but he panted to the surface a few yards downstream, pressed against a rock.

He looked up and saw an eagle circling high up above him in a cloudless sky.

He watched for a long time, one with the eagle and one with the river, then he waded to the bank, and climbed out into the burning sunshine, still half numb with the cold, but cleansed and new.

When Stephen had arrived in Delhi it was unbelievably

227

hot. Even the flies could hardly stir themselves from the ceiling at midday, and his memories of the journey down from Afghanistan and through Pakistan were already obliterated by the sheer difficulty of taking the next breath. People, places drifted into his consciousness for a while and then receded into the heat haze. He had no plan beyond a vague idea of going to Benares; Jerry had talked about it – it sounded an interesting place. He travelled with other Westerners, but he had no constant friend and needed none.

India was confusing at first, so different from the countries he had come through: the crowds, the beautiful women in gorgeously coloured saris, the cows in the streets, the bicycle rickshaws, the monkeys on the roof-tops, the temples with their garish idols, the sweet smells of incense mingled with cow-dung, and the ever-present, overpowering heat.

When he had the energy to think at all, he yearned for the simplicity of a mosque and the wide spaces of the desert.

In a dirty boarding house near the city centre, he heard there was a village a few miles out of Delhi where you could stay cheaply in a half-ruined Mughal palace, so he took a bus there. It was just as hot, but the ruins were beautiful and the air was clean, and in the afternoon you could sit under the mango tree, smoking chillums and occasionally cooling yourself with a bucket of water straight from the well.

He had no sense of where he might be going any more, and no plans. It was too hot for plans.

At night the temperature dropped a few degrees, a breeze rustled the mango leaves and moonlight flooded the overgrown gardens. It was impossibly beautiful. He went for a walk and saw a little fire, and approached it. That was how he met Mukhtibaba.

Since arriving in India, Stephen had seen plenty of Sadhus, wandering holy men, half naked – sometimes completely naked – daubed with ash, and with matted hair and long beards. Among all the other strange sights he hadn't taken much notice. He was growing used to strangeness. Mukhtibaba was sitting with two other Sadhus beside a Hindu shrine. He looked up towards Stephen and called to him:

'Hello! Yes! Come on! Chillum!'

Stephen never knew how much English Mukhtibaba could really speak, probably more than he let on. He communicated sparingly with words, but as they shared a chillum Stephen looked into his eyes and felt a coming together at a huge depth, an instant, effortless meeting of minds, as if beyond the vast cultural gap they had always known each other.

The fire flickered. The two other Sadhus sat cross-legged, silent but very present. Mukhtibaba grinned at Stephen through toothless gums.

'You coming with me. I teach you. You my *chela*.'

They left Delhi together and headed towards the mountains, never hurrying, pausing at every shrine but never stopping for more than a day. They took trains and buses, and for long distances they walked, sometimes in company with other Sadhus, more often just the two of them. They slept in *dharmsalas* – rest-houses provided free for pilgrims – or beside temples. They smoked chillums constantly. Mukhtibaba smiled and laughed a lot, in contrast to most of the other Sadhus who were often grim and blunt, but usually he spoke little, though he took care to instruct Stephen in the right etiquette: to keep the fire clean; to make tea with the proper spices, and chapattis so that they blew up like balloons; to pay respect to other Sadhus by sitting straight-backed in the lotus position however stoned you were, and never pointing your feet towards them or – Heaven forbid! – blowing smoke in their faces; to keep your own cloth for the chillum and clean it properly after use. Stephen's contribution was to buy the hash – often simply from a shop in a village. Mukhtibaba or his comrades begged food and cooked meals that were always delicious.

When Mukhtibaba did speak at any length, it was usually about his gods. He taught Stephen to call invocations to Shiva before lighting a chillum, and to chant mantras deep in his throat so that the vibrations filled him. Whenever they passed a shrine to Ganesh, the elephant-headed son of Shiva and Parvati to whom he had a special devotion, he stopped and performed rituals. He pointed out images of Kali, the goddess of death and destruction, whose mouth foams with blood and who rides a tiger. He also talked about *Kundalini* – the life force that lies coiled like a snake at the base of the spine – and showed Stephen some of the techniques of yogic breathing known as *pranayama*. Stephen enjoyed the breathing exercises, but much of the rest washed over him. For him, the mystical road that they walked on was enough, his eyes opened by the hashish and the company of the Baba to an ancientness beyond imagining, a landscape within a landscape, and a way of life that disappeared back into the mists of time.

'You not thinking!' Mukhtibaba would instruct him. 'Foreign people always thinking, thinking. Thinking, you can never see,' and he pointed to the spot on his forehead where a third eye would be.

Whether Mukhtibaba had a third eye, Stephen wasn't sure, but he soon realised the hypnotic power that was in his normal eyes. And through the Baba's company, he felt the same power growing in his own.

They bathed in the Ganges at Haridwar, then went on up through the jungle into the Himalayas. Even here the days were blisteringly hot, but at night the air was cooler. Occasionally Stephen caught a sight of snow-capped mountains – the high peaks of the Garwhal, where the Ganges has its source.

The cave had been cut long ago by hand into the rock at the side of a valley, where a stream flowed down from a plateau. In the centre of the cave was a *lingam*, the phallic-shaped stone that symbolises the power of Shiva, and orange paste was smeared on the walls. Iron tridents were stacked at the entrance as symbolic offerings. This was a place of power, and Stephen felt it instantly – not like the spaciousness of the mosques, but a buzzing intensity. Outside, there was a sort of terrace with a fireplace, sheltered by the overhanging rock, that had been levelled with a smooth surface of mud and cow-dung, and maintained perhaps for centuries by Sadhus who had stayed a few days, or a few years, and passed on.

Mukhtibaba put down his bedroll and sat on it. He was puffed from the climb. He grinned up at Stephen.

'Making tea.' It was an instruction.

The fireplace was still warm. The last occupants of the cave had not long gone. Stephen dug down into the ashes and brought up hot embers and with a few sticks blew up a fire. Mukhtibaba had told him that there were Sadhu fires – *dhunis* they were called – that had never been extinguished for a thousand years.

He fetched water from the stream. The forest was around him and the sky was above him; he was lean and fit and very stoned, and life was everywhere, but especially here.

Later, as evening approached, the headman from a neighbouring village arrived with an offering of rice and vegetables, which Mukhtibaba accepted gravely. The headman looked impressed by the white-skinned, blond-haired *chela*. In India, Stephen realised, true seekers after God would never go hungry.

They stayed for three days. Once some villagers came to talk with Mukhtibaba about their problems, but otherwise they were left alone. The Baba spent a lot of time in the cave, meditating or performing rituals, which remained as

232

obscure as ever to Stephen. Mukhtibaba made no effort to explain them. Three Sadhus, including a woman, appeared out of the jungle on the second evening, and sat late into the night round the fire smoking and talking in Hindi with Mukhtibaba, whom they treated with respect. When Stephen woke in the morning they had already gone.

When he was not cleaning the cave or making the tea or washing clothes (the Baba insisted on high standards of cleanliness), Stephen wandered in the jungle watching the birds and the white monkeys that seemed to have their home nearby, and wondering if he would meet anything more threatening, like a bear or a leopard. But the nearest he came to that was a King Cobra, that looked at him for a long minute before gliding gently past him as he stood still, amazed by its power and beauty.

He told Mukhtibaba about the cobra.

'Very good!' he nodded. 'Auspicious omen!'

That afternoon, the third day they had been there, the Baba took Stephen into the deepest part of the cave, behind the lingam. It was cool and dark and smelt of incense. Mukhtibaba was chanting softly. Stephen effortlessly sunk inside himself, as he often did in Mukhtibaba's company, and felt as though he was on a pillow of coloured lights and soft vibrations.

He had no idea how long he sat there, but when Mukhtibaba coughed and brought him gently back, he stepped out of the cave into a world of soft light and lengthening shadows. Mukhtibaba made the tea himself, which was unusual, and packed a chillum with his best Manali *charas*, which he reserved for special occasions.

There was a strange, powerful energy; a blood red sunset, and then the full moon rising.

Stephen cleaned the chillum. Now that he smoked regularly, the hash had less effect than it used to, but he realised he was very stoned.

'Good!' said Mukhtibaba. 'We go on!'

Stephen sat again in the back of the cave, but this time the Baba's chanting had changed and seemed full of dissonance, repetitive, irritating. It was all Stephen could do to remain sittting up, and he abandoned his straight back and let his shoulders hunch. His whole body was tired and painful, and he longed to lie down, but he knew Mukhtibaba would be displeased, and he was in truth a little afraid of him. For the first time, he began to doubt Mukhtibaba's sanity, or at least his own part in this adventure. What on earth was he doing here, half way up the Himalayas with a heathen idolator? He shut his eyes, but there were no swirling lights or beatific visions, just thoughts, a great flood of them that he could no longer keep back . . .

He had no business here. He was not a Hindu. What did the Baba want from him? And what did he want from the Baba? It was all nonsense, he could suddenly see that clearly, and even if it wasn't it had nothing to do with him. He was in the wrong place. A shaft of worry hit him, about his money. He only had a few dollars left – what would he do when it had gone? He should be back in

England. He should have gone home ages ago, while he still could, after he had seen Rob on the bus, got on with his life, gone back to school...

The Baba's chanting became more intense.

Back to school. He saw at once the meaninglessness, the absurdity; the emptiness of his whole life. There as well as here. Back to school. Back to school. Back to school. It was like a mantra repeating itself in his head. But he would never go back to school. Never. School was death of the soul.

A face appeared in the darkness in front of him. He knew it was only his imagination, but it was so real he felt he could have touched it: Mr Wortle, smiling, his lips parted to show his tongue touching his teeth. With an effort, Stephen made him disappear. He knew he could do it, but it required a focus he had never summoned before. Utterly concentrated, he watched the face dissolve, like the Cheshire Cat, very slowly, the smile last.

Stephen's back straightened. He felt victorious.

He allowed himself to remember, briefly, the last three weeks of the term, the drive in silence back to the college, throbbing with shame, and the conspiratorial look of consummated lust Mr Wortle gave him as he left his car. Then every English lesson was a torture of trying to avoid Mr Wortle's eyes – those big, deep eyes that had once seemed so kind and understanding – finding excuses not to go to the Aesthetes, to avoid, to avoid, while always tempted: the lure of forbidden pleasures that he dreaded and desired at the same time.

All that was over now. Whenever he wanted, he would make Mr Wortle disappear, slowly, smile last.

The chanting had stopped. The cave was deeply silent. Mukhtibaba stood up and came over to him.

Stephen kept his eyes shut – not that he could have seen anything anyway; the cave was completely dark by now. He felt light and fully alert again, his head rising as if pulled by a string, his back finding a new looseness and straightness.

In silence, Mukhtibaba touched Stephen on the forehead. As he did so, Stephen experienced a sudden rush of energy that seemed to release itself from the base of his spine, shoot upwards through his spinal cord and explode in his head in coloured lights, filling him with a sense of perfect bliss. Then, behind the bliss, nothing. Emptiness as vast as the universe.

This was it. He was here. He remained suspended, all fear dispersed from his being, knowing only that he had tasted the un-nameable, and that nothing would ever be the same again.

At last, Mukhtibaba chuckled.

'Very good! Now you know Kundalini! Now you live, no problem. Now you go.'

He touched Stephen gently on the eyelids.

Then they went outside and made chapattis under the full moon.

Stephen woke in the early morning. Mukhtibaba was still sleeping on his bedroll beside the embers of the fire.

Stephen looked at him. He had never seen him asleep before, and there was a vulnerability about the Baba's face that he had never noticed when he was awake. Mukhtibaba had no need of Stephen though. He was sufficient in himself, and he had told Stephen to go. And now Stephen had no need of him. He loved him with undying gratitude, he had received the greatest gift in the world from him, and yet in another way he hardly knew him. How could you know someone so dedicated to his own dissolution? Anyway, personal relationships meant nothing to Stephen now. He was free in a way that previously he could not even have imagined.

Already the events of the night before were fading in his memory, because there was nothing to remember except a rush of bliss. Yet Stephen knew that he had finished what he came here for, that from now on his life would be utterly different, rooted in the moment, and that he should go.

He picked up his bag and his blanket. Then he took out three dollar bills, the last of the money he had made selling Jerry's hash, and pushed them under Mukhtibaba's bedroll. The Baba would probably just give them away himself, but that didn't matter.

'*Namaste, Babaji*,' he muttered.

Without looking round he walked down the track, back to the world.

Five days later he stood in the Ganges near Rishikesh, tore up his passport and watched it float away down the river.

Chapter 19

Stephen had found that in India, the more bizarre his dress and behaviour by the standards of home, the less notice anyone took of him. He walked half naked down the river bank towards the ashram town of Rishikesh, his blanket slung over his shoulder and his few possesssions in a cotton bag, unremarked. Ahead of him he could see a crowd gathered around a Western couple trying to take a photograph of a temple.

He decided to speak to them. He was curious to hear his own voice again. He walked up to them and the crowd parted to let him through.

'Hello,' he said. 'Can I help?'

They stared at him. They were an attractive pair in their early twenties, with pink, pleasant faces. The girl had a straw hat and a floral dress. The boy wore loose Indian trousers and a Western shirt.

'Are you – er – English?' asked the boy.

'I was,' said Stephen, catching the boy's gaze and holding his eyes with his own for a few moments – just long enough for the boy to feel his power.

The girl tossed her head.

'These people are such a hassle. I wish they'd leave us alone,' she said crossly.

Stephen met her eyes too. They tried to flicker away and she blinked several times before he felt her.

She was pretty, but he preferred the boy.

He turned to the Indian kids, gathered in a circle and grinning at the free entertainment.

'*Jaó! Chaló! Jaldí!*' he commanded.

They hesitated, but there was something about him and they fell back.

'Thanks,' said the boy. 'It's such a drag being surrounded all the time. We hardly dare go out sometimes.'

'And the beggars!' said the girl. 'It's a disgrace. Why don't they do something about them?'

Stephen said nothing. He was a beggar himself, now. His silence made them uncomfortable.

'Have you been here a long time?' asked the boy.

'No. I just arrived here, as you saw.'

'I meant, in India,' said the boy awkwardly. 'I mean, you can speak the language and things...'

'I don't know much Hindi. Anyway it's easy. You could learn enough to get by on in a couple of days if you chose.'

He was already bored with them, though the boy was rather sweet, with a gentle mouth. He caught his eye again and smiled at him. Then he cupped his hands and bowed his head in a gesture of farewell, and turned to leave.

'Where are you going?' the girl called after him. He ignored her.

'Hang on a minute,' said the boy. 'Why don't we go for a chai?'

Stephen paused.

'I have no money,' he said.

'We'll buy you one,' said the boy. 'Obviously.'

★

239

'How can you live without any money?' asked the girl.

They were sitting in a tiny chai-shop overlooking the river bank. The sun had disappeared behind clouds that had spread out suddenly from the mountains.

'I need little,' said Stephen. 'And India is kind.'

'But how do you eat?' the girl insisted. 'What did you eat yesterday?'

'I ate at the Gurudwara of a Sikh temple. They feed all pilgrims.'

'And tomorrow?'

He smiled.

'Who knows? God will provide.'

How could they understand, though? They'd never understand the purity and power that came from having no possessions, no past, no future – total insecurity.

'Where are you staying?' asked the boy, with his gentle voice.

Stephen looked at him. Sleeping was the easiest part; there were rest-houses and temples all over India where anyone could sleep for free, and failing that you could put down your blanket anywhere. But this couple would know nothing of that. They had money and luggage to protect.

'Last night I was in a cave further up the Ganges,' he said. 'I shared it with a cobra.'

'Oh my God!' said the girl, putting her hand to her mouth.

'It was all right. I didn't bother him and he didn't bother me.'

The boy was awed by him, he could tell that. The girl was fascinated but a bit repelled.

Stephen hummed an '*Om*' deep in his throat, the way Mukhtibaba used to, barely audible to anyone else, yet filling his body with vibration. He made eye contact with the boy, then let his eyes unfocus, while still holding him with his gaze. He felt the boy suck into him again. He could do anything with him, he knew. Take him away from this stupid girl, that would be a start . . .

He was sixteen. He had no idea what date it was, so he didn't know when his birthday had been, but by now it must have been well past, together with the O-level exams. But that was all rubbish. He had no age any more. No nationality. No identity.

He refocused his eyes and blinked. Then he smiled. The boy smiled back.

'Human kind cannot bear very much reality,' said Stephen, but neither of them understood the reference. He took out his hash – it was almost the last he had, but God would provide – and filled a chillum, taking his time.

'What *is* real?' asked the boy, surprisingly.

Stephen paused, then he gestured at the chai-shop owner, an old man who sat cross-legged behind his stove polishing his five tea-glasses. The chai-shop was made of mud and straw and drift wood, but it was immaculately clean. It was built among the rocks at the edge of the Ganges, which had risen in the last few days and flowed a few yards away. When the monsoon rains came, which would be soon, the chai-shop would become part of the river.

'Is *he* real?' said Stephen. 'I think so, don't you?'

The boy nodded.

'Yes,' he said. 'The old man's about as real as it's possible to be.'

The girl was agitated. She talked to hide it.

'We were staying at that big ashram up the hill,' she said. 'Studying yoga. But we didn't like it. The food was weird and the Swami was really creepy. He kept making passes at Will. So we've moved to the tourist bungalow. We're going to Benares tomorrow, see what that's like. I bet it'll be hot though.'

Hot. Yes, it would certainly be hot. Even here with the mountain breezes, the heat was oppressive, though for the last few days the clouds had gathered in the afternoon. As they sat, there was a flash and a thunderclap from the hills. It would probably rain in a while, the big drops cooling and soothing, and everybody hoped for it.

'*Om Shiva!*' intoned Stephen, as a fork of lightning crackled down into the jungle on the hillside opposite.

He handed Will the packed chillum, inviting him to light it.

The girl looked alarmed.

'Will!' she said. 'I don't think you should!'

Stephen half closed his eyes and withdrew into himself, swaying gently and feeling the vibrations pulsing up and down his spine.

'Stop hassling me,' said Will, looking at her furiously.

The vibrations in Stephen's spine danced with a little more energy. He struck two matches and held them to

242

the chillum. The boy sucked, coughed vigorously, and handed it back. Stephen drew on it smoothly. The vibrations in his spine intensified, and then grew spaces. He moved his consciousness up and down his spine, remembering Mukhtibaba.

'Never think! Thinking bad,' the Baba had said, and since his experience in the cave, Stephen understood what he meant. Now, with the last link severed from his past, the thinking would surely all stop for good, and there was no limit to how high he could go.

He offered the chillum to the girl, assuming she would refuse, but she took it and puffed half-heartedly; she didn't want to be left out, but wasn't willing to really come in. The boy was already well stoned, gazing raptly at some vultures picking at the remains of a dead dog on the river bank.

He would make the boy his disciple, he decided. His first. The girl would have to go.

But she was smiling at him. She was stoned, and she was smiling at him, trying to be friendly.

'What's your name? We never even told each other our names, yet,' she said, with a sudden warmth.

'Stephen.'

It came out before he had thought about it, or he would have found himself a new name, a better one for his new state of being. But there it was, so that was how it was meant to be.

'Too much!' she laughed. 'My name's Stephanie – Steph – so we've got the same name. Where are you going to stay tonight?'

Stephen shrugged, and gestured at the blanket over his shoulder.

'Wherever I am,' he said.

The boy – Will – was swaying backwards and forwards and staring into space. The vultures were still picking at the dog, but he had lost interest. Stephanie touched him on the shoulder.

'Are you all right, Will?' she asked. 'This is how he gets when he's stoned,' she explained to Stephen. 'It's like his brain stops working. It freaks me out.'

Stephen turned Will towards him, looking in his eyes, which gradually focused in on his own.

'Will!' he said. Then he coughed, a sharp bark like the Baba used to make. 'Will!'

The boy twitched, then blinked and looked around, bewildered.

'Oh, yeah,' said Will. 'I was . . . I don't know . . .'

'Drink some chai,' said Stephen, and the boy put the glass to his mouth and sipped obediently.

There was another crackle of lightning. The rain would definitely come soon.

'We'd better get back to the tourist bungalow,' said Stephanie. 'If Will can still walk, that is . . . Hey, I've got an idea: why don't you come back with us? We could buy you a meal and things . . .'

He made love to Stephanie that night, in her bed, while Will slept off the effects of the chillum. Afterwards she held him very tight as he lay immobile, his breath slowed

244

to almost nothing, immersed in the coloured lights of the astral plane.

All the power of the universe was his, to use as he chose.

The next day Will and Stephanie paid for Stephen's train ticket to go with them to Benares.

Even at dawn the heat was intense. It was imposssible to sleep on the tight-packed, claustrophobic train, and they were all relieved to be out of it, standing on the station platform in the first grey light.

'I wonder if there's such a thing as a hotel with air-conditioning,' said Stephanie.

'First we bathe,' said Stephen.

They followed the crowds of pilgrims through the narrow, filthy streets of the old bazaar, that was just coming awake. Then suddenly they emerged, and there in front of them was a huge expanse of water: the Ganges, the same river that Stephen had thrown his passport into, but not a gushing mountain torrent any more, but a calm expanse of water half a kilometre wide. Stepped terraces – the famous *ghats* of Benares – led down to the water, where the pilgrims bathed and floated paper boats with candles and incense. Holy men sat cross-legged in shadowy recesses, and sitar music and chanting drifted in from the temples.

Will and Stephanie stood awkwardly with their big rucksacks as Stephen dropped his bag, ran forward with the crowd, and plunged in.

The water was blissfully refreshing and a wave of deep

happiness passed through him. This must have been how the great sages felt, the Enlightened Masters, all down the ages...

The sun rose above the murk on the horizon and around him a thousand pilgrims chanted their invocations to their gods.

He walked slowly out, to rejoin Stephanie and Will. He would allow them to care for him for a few days. In return, he would teach them the beauty of non-attachment. He was filled with a great love of all beings, but with a special fondness for them, his first disciples.

On the steps at the water's edge he stretched himself, and let the water drip off him. The sun was already hot, and would soon dry him. He was as clean and perfect as the morning.

'Bull*shit*! What the fuck are you doing here?'

He turned to the voice, startled, but before he saw the face, he already knew for certain who it was.

Chapter 20

In front of him stood Rob.

Stephen felt a panic. Of all people, he was not ready to see Rob. After that fleeting vision in Afghanistan, he had realised he never wanted to see him again. He had no need of him now.

He tried to steady his breath, desperately trying to hang on to those blissful sensations of a few moments ago. Perhaps he could lose himself in the crowd, disappear, until he recovered his sense of oneness.

But it was too late. Rob was already there.

Rob looked older, and seemed shorter than Stephen remembered him. His skin was very brown and his eyes were fierce. He had shaved and had his hair cropped short, leaving a single lock at the back, in the Brahmin fashion. He hardly seemed like the brother Stephen had known in England, but he was. He was. He still had a cracked tooth, and his voice was unmistakable.

'What the fuck are you doing here, Stevie?' he asked again. The crowd had given way for him and they were face to face.

Stephen had no answer. Adrenaline was pumping through him and the back of his mouth was dry.

All at once, Rob's features softened into a smile, and he put an arm on Stephen's shoulder and grasped it affectionately.

'Anyway, it *is* you! I saw you in Kabul, didn't I, as my

247

bus left? I thought you were a ghost then, but you're real, I think.'

Stephen opened his mouth to say something, trying to think of something clever, something that would make him feel in control again, but the best he could manage was,

'Hi, Rob!'

But as he said it he looked in Rob's eyes, and suddenly he couldn't help smiling. Suddenly they were brothers again.

'Well, we'd better talk,' said Rob. 'Come to my place.'

Stephen hesitated, remembering Will and Stephanie. He could see them from the corner of his eye, standing awkwardly with their bulky rucksacks.

'I've got friends.'

'Where?'

They went over to them. Will was watching the scene with dreamy eyes and his mouth half open, but Stephanie was irritated.

'I've just met—' Stephen started to explain.

'Look, we've been waiting around a long time here, and we want to go and find a hotel now,' complained Stephanie.

'Fuck off to your hotel then,' said Rob contemptuously. 'Come on, Stevie.' He turned and walked away up the ghats.

Stephen hesitated. Stephanie looked upset, and he didn't want to leave them like this. But he'd find them again when he wanted them.

'He's my brother. I have to talk to him. See you later.'

He hitched his bag over his shoulder and followed Rob.

The yellow sun hovering over the fields on the other side of the river was already blindingly hot, and the pilgrims were dispersing, going home, or to their jobs – anywhere out of the sun.

Rob led Stephen down a back street, then through a scruffy courtyard with a pump and children playing, and pushed open a door.

'My room,' he said. 'Come on in.'

It was dark and dirty, and just as untidy as Stephen would have expected. An electric fan turned slowly in a ceiling lost in cobwebs and grime, and on the floor a thin cotton mattress was strewn with dirty clothes. There was a sort of table, improvised from an old door and some bricks, and littered with books, bits of paper, defunct biros, torn-up cigarettes, and peanut shells. The only thing that looked clean was a sitar, propped carefully against the wall.

Stephen could hear his mother in his head:

'Rob! Clean up your room this instant!'

Rob never did.

'Chai?' asked Rob, putting a saucepan onto a dilapidated kerosene stove. He made the tea in the Indian way, boiling up the tea leaves with the milk and sugar, though without the care that Stephen had learned from Mukhtibaba. Stephen cleared himself a space on the mattress and sat in the lotus position. He was quite calm now; he could feel his breath moving smoothly through his nose. It was only Rob after all. His big brother. He would talk to him, tell him what he had always meant to tell him. That was what this meeting was for.

'What are you up to here, then?' asked Stephen.

'Learning sitar, actually,' said Rob. 'I've got a teacher here. You would not believe the depth there is in Indian music, Stevie. It's like poetry without the words. I'll never be any fucking good at it of course, but it's teaching me to hear.'

Rob handed a glass of tea to Stephen.

'So. What about you? What are you doing here? You didn't come to look for me, did you?'

Stephen took a sip of his tea before replying.

'Why don't you ever write to Mum and Dad, Rob? Why not just send them a card to let them know where you are?'

Rob tossed his head in annoyance.

'What's all that shit about? They don't own me. They know I've got my own life to live – I'll go and see them one day, when I'm ready.'

'Mum thinks you're dead.'

'BULLSHIT!'

It was like an explosion. Rob jerked forward, his face tense with anger.

'Is that what she told you? What she tells everyone? That woman is all lies, Stevie. She knows I'm not dead. I wrote to her from Ibiza, a long letter, told her where I was going, why I wanted to get away. I told her not to expect to hear for a while . . . Did she tell you that? Huh? Did she tell you that?'

No. She hadn't said that. Not to him, not to the police, not to anybody. Stephen hesitated, flustered.

'Maybe she didn't get the letter...'

'Of course she got the fucking letter. Did she call the police?'

Stephen nodded.

'That was for *your* benefit, you know that? Yours and the old man, maybe. So that you'd never dare to do what I did!'

Rob suddenly relaxed and sat back smiling. He sipped his tea.

'It didn't work though, by the look of it. Had the opposite effect, maybe. Because here you are. And welcome, Stevie. Welcome to India. It's good to see you again.'

Stephen smiled back. This was the old Rob, a Rob he remembered now, full of explosions and sudden warmth. As for his mother – well, Rob was probably right, but it was all a long way away. None of that mattered now.

'Yes,' he said. 'I'm glad to see you too, Rob.'

For a moment the warmth of brothers hung in the air between them as they drank their tea and smiled.

'I am surprised, though,' Rob continued. 'Aren't you supposed to be doing your O-levels or something? What happened? *She* didn't send you here, did she?'

'No. Mum never mentioned you any more. I was on my way to France, and I met a guy called Jerry, who said he knew you.'

'Jerry? Like, Jerry and Astrid?'

'Jerry and Astrid. Yes. They were on the ferry.'

251

'Astrid too. Gorgeous chick, eh? I bet you fell in love with her, didn't you? Everybody does. It does Jerry's nut in, though he's too cool to show it! She's a fantastic lay, too. Hey, did you sleep with her, bro?'

Rob leant forward towards him, grinning. Stephen could feel his adrenaline rising again, but he stopped it with a couple of breaths. He was in control now. Rob wouldn't blow him off course again.

'Look, I don't want to talk about that, Rob.'

Rob raised an eyebrow.

'Okay. Fine,' he said, lying back against the wall and starting to roll a joint. 'I knew Jerry was in Benares actually, because I saw him yesterday down on the ghats. Did he bring you all the way here?'

'No...' said Stephen, momentarily taken aback by the information. But Jerry was nothing to him now. He pulled up his legs and straightened his back.

'No. They gave me a lift to Istanbul, and then I found my own way. It's true that I was looking for you at first, but I gave up on that long ago. I travel for myself and my own wisdom.'

Rob threw back his head and laughed. He was always moving, Stephen noticed. He could never be still.

'Hark at you! "*I travel for myself and my own wisdom.*" You're fifteen, Stevie, don't come on at me like some fucking yogi.'

'Sixteen, actually.'

'Oh, yeah, I forgot! Let's have a cake for you, shall we? Sixteen candles, and all sing "Happy Birthday!" What were you doing in France anyway?'

'I had a French exchange with a boy called Thierry in Charleville.'

Rob almost jumped up in excitement.

'Charleville! Are you serious? Charleville? You should have gone there, Stevie. That's where Rimbaud came from.'

'What?'

'Rimbaud. You know, the poet: *The Drunken Boat, A Season in Hell.* Charleville – that's where he was born, and grew up, where he wrote his poems. If it was in India there'd be a temple to him. Being Europe I guess there's a museum.'

'*I is someone else* – was that Rimbaud?'

'It certainly was. How did you learn that? From Mr Wortle?'

Stephen nodded.

'Yeah,' Rob continued. 'Mr Wortle. The Wart! Grindlesham College . . . What a world! I'll tell you something, though, Stevie, I owe one hell of a lot to that guy, because he showed me what poetry is, and I do realise now that in all the darkness of that shithole, he is the one little ray of light. Did he teach you? He is the only good thing about that fucking school, and if you ever go back you can thank him for me.'

Stephen squirmed. He had to tell Rob, he could see that, as he had always planned to. But not for his own sake – he was beyond that sort of need – but for Rob's.

'Yes he did teach me,' he said coldly. 'And I need to tell you something, Rob.'

Rob was rolling a joint, licking the cigarette paper. He caught something in Stephen's voice and looked up expectantly, waiting for him to speak.

But the words wouldn't come. Stephen's mouth had gone dry, and a mosquito was droning over his head. The heat was overwhelming.

He couldn't say it. He'd been wrong – Rob wouldn't understand at all. He'd laugh and make fun of it. Or he'd refuse to believe it.

He wiped the sweat from his forehead with his hand.

'Yes?' said Rob, still watching him.

'You know, Mr Wortle...' started Stephen. Then he stopped.

It belonged to another life. His past had washed away into the Ganges with his passport. It was none of Rob's business after all.

'Well?'

'I met a Baba in Rishikesh,' said Stephen smoothly. 'He took me into the jungle and raised my Kundalini.'

Rob grunted, unimpressed, and looked back down at his joint as if he had lost interest.

'Did he try and fuck you?'

He lit the joint.

'No,' said Stephen. 'He taught me mantras and—'

'They usually do,' Rob cut in. 'Could be a good experience if you're into it. I guess this one was more into girls. Or chillums. Where have you left all your stuff, anyway? With those two creepy tourists you arrived here with?'

Stephen gestured to his shoulder bag.

'This is all I have.'

Rob blew out smoke and stared at him wide-eyed.

'Christ! You *are* on some kind of trip, aren't you?'

Stephen half closed his eyes and felt himself back into the vibrations in his spine. He had had enough of Rob. Rob was his past and his past was nothing. He would compose himself, and then he would go.

Rob slumped back and watched him, drawing on his joint.

'You got any money?'

'No. I don't need money. I gave it away.'

'YOU GAVE IT AWAY? For Christ's sake – who do you think you are? Jesus, or something? Get real, Stevie, you don't get far without money in India, or anywhere else for that matter. You know what – when I saw you out of that bus window, I did not know what I was seeing. No kidding. I thought I was hallucinating. There was my little brother dressed like an Afghani tribesman and waving at me like I was on a train to Reading. I had definitely been doing too much opium. You made me give it up, you know that? You made me give up the opium. Too much shit!'

He laughed, and dragged on his joint again, before handing it to Stephen.

'You don't do a lot of drugs, do you? Just a hash smoker with a little chillum, right? But I've done it all – acid, opium, morphine, datura – it all works, but you know what? There is nothing that scrambles your brains like alcohol. Have you ever tried the local liquor? Don't!

Total annihilation. Too much of that and you really are fucked for good.'

He laughed again. Stephen held the joint without smoking it. He wasn't interested in Rob's drug-taking. He would leave as soon as Rob stopped talking.

'India's a funny place. It's kind of puritanical about sex, but there are people here who really understand what intoxication is about. It's not about Fun. It's not about having a Good Time – it's about God! Shiva! You destroy your mind, you blot out your thought, and you see. You see. The price is high, but you see. It's not for you, though, Stevie. I'm telling you now. It's not for you. Because I'm the fucking nutcase in our family, and you are basically sane, good and intelligent with a bright future ahead of you and you don't know how lucky you are.'

He looked at Stephen intently, speaking quietly and seriously.

'You should go back, you know. They need you. Mum and Dad. They need you.'

'They needed you.'

'No they didn't. I was nothing but their show pony, and surprise, surprise I have my own life to live. But you are different. Go back home, Stevie. Because you're too young, and this isn't your place, and that little Sadhu act you've got going wouldn't fool anybody... except maybe that couple of idiots you came here with. Go back to Mum and say you're sorry and get your hair cut and pass your exams. Go back to Grindlesham. Go and learn more poetry from Mr Wortle. I'll get you the money. I've got friends here...we'll get you an airline ticket.'

Stephen put down the joint on a piece of slate that seemed to be there for the purpose, and stood up. He would not get angry. It wasn't worth reacting. Rob could only ever see him as his little brother, because that was his conditioning. That was Rob's problem. Stephen would just leave, because there was no point in staying.

'Actually, Rob, I can't go home, because I don't have a passport,' he said casually, heading for the door.

'What?'

'I tore my passport up and threw it in the Ganges. Go home yourself if it's so important to you!'

Stephen turned the door handle, strong in his own superiority.

'There's something else, isn't there?' said Rob softly behind him.

Stephen paused without turning.

'I know I haven't been very nice to you, Stevie. I never was, really, was I? It's not how I want to be, I can't help it. But I'm your brother and I see you as you are, and I know you didn't come all this way just to tell me you'd torn up your passport. You were looking for me, Stevie. Now you've found me. Don't go. I'm here.'

Outside, the children were shouting. Stephen stood looking at the door. He had wanted to talk to Rob. It was true. There was so much he had wanted to share with him. But it was over now. It was too late...

'It's not too late,' said Rob. 'It's never too late.'

Stephen felt his spine sag and a huge weariness settle

257

on his shoulders. It was the weight of his past, and it was Rob, and the way Rob could always make him feel bad about himself. The weariness would lift again if he only could just get out of the door, find Stephanie and Will, who made him feel good about himself. But first he would say what he had to say, and then he would be free.

With one hand on the door, he turned to face Rob, and with an effort drew himself up straight.

'You're right,' he said. 'I do have something to tell you. About the Wart – Mr Wortle, your hero. He buggered me. Took me to a hotel and buggered me stupid. I expect you think that's great, just like your Rimbaud. That's it. Goodbye.'

The children in the courtyard were pouring water over each other. They stopped and stared at him as he passed.

In a minute he was lost in the crowded streets.

Chapter 21

It was unbearably hot – close and sticky, with no wind, so that the sweat dripped off him. The city was wrapped in a haze of pollution. Even Stephen's breath came heavily. All through the middle of the day he stayed near the river, bathing and then resting in the shade, and drinking water from a pump provided for pilgrims. It was impossible, though, to get comfortable. Then, when the sun dropped lower and most of the streets were in shade, he went in search of Stephanie and Will.

He had not eaten since the night before, and he was hungry.

He looked in several tourist hotels near the ghats, but there was no sign of them and the people he met were tense and unfriendly – one hotel keeper even shouted at him to go away. He sat in a tourist restaurant expecting to strike up a conversation or at least be bought a chai, but nobody took any notice of him except the restaurant owner who gave him dirty looks. Everyone was pre-occupied with their own business.

He returned to the ghats, as the fading light began to offer a respite from the heat. There would be no problem about sleeping on the ghats. He could lay down his blanket anywhere and no one would disturb him.

A group of Sadhus, silhouetted in a little huddle against the violet sky, beckoned him over.

'Chillum?'

But they were not offering him a chillum, they were asking him for some hash to put in theirs, and his supply had run out. When they realised this they lost interest in him.

He lay down by a temple, using his bag for a pillow, feeling the emptiness in his stomach and hearing the night sounds of the city: the river lapping against the steps, sitar music and chanting, shouted invocations to Shiva from the chillum smokers.

He was outside it all now, alone and unwanted.

He didn't care. Jesus also had been betrayed.

Mosquitoes were humming around him, waiting for their chance to settle. If he pulled his blanket over his head they bit his feet, if he pulled it back down over his feet, they attacked his face.

The stone was hard.

He fell asleep in the end, and then was woken by a dog sniffing at him. He shooed it off. The night was very still and very dark, with no stars. The mosquitoes had taken their fill and gone away.

Then, just before dawn, the temperature dropped to the almost pleasant, and the crowds of pilgrims arrived for their ritual bath in the Ganges. Blearily he picked himself up and went with the crowd down to the water's edge. He felt too weak and tired to go right in, so he just dipped his feet in and picked up a little water with his hands and put it to his forehead, asking a blessing of Mother Ganga.

There was no sunrise. Black clouds had moved in

overnight, and all that happened was that the light grew stronger and the temperature rose. Everyone looked up at the clouds, with relief and anticipation. The rains were coming.

As Stephen came out of the water, he thought he saw Rob again, this time together with Jerry. They were scanning the crowds, but they were too far away to call to. Not that he wanted to see Rob again anyway.

As the crowds dispersed, he returned to where he had slept, and sat there, next to a group of Nagas – naked Sadhus. They appeared to have no belongings, not even clothes, and their bodies were smeared with ash to protect them from the sun and the insects. A few weeks ago he would have found them both exotic and frightening, but now he felt drawn to them and the purity of their lives. He would have liked to join them, but they took no notice of him.

Soon, he was sure, Stephanie and Will would turn up. They would be looking for him. Or if not them, then someone else would come – Jerry perhaps. Or even Mary and Ian. Or new people would recognise his wisdom, and care for him. God would provide, as He always had.

With the overcast sky, the heat was more bearable. In the afternoon, Stephen fell asleep and dreamed of his mother. She was baking a cake. She opened the oven, and took out a Victoria sponge, perfect and already filled with jam and whipped cream. The smell was more beautiful than anything Stephen had ever known. She smiled at him, tight-lipped, and cut a big piece and handed it to him. His mouth was watering. He took a huge bite out of the cake. But it tasted like ashes and he spat it out, wanting to vomit.

He looked at his mother. She was still smiling at him, but her lips parted, and a worm crawled out between them.

'Mum!' he called to her. 'You've got a worm.'

She threw back her head and laughed uproariously, and her wide open mouth was full of maggots.

He woke up with a new kind of gnawing hunger. This would not wait any longer. He must eat. He would beg, like the Sadhus did.

He took his bowl from his bag and walked to the food stalls. He held out his bowl, and the stallholders laughed at the white beggar and dropped in some bits of rice and old chapatti. One gave a healthy dollop of lentils, saying something to his friends in Hindi. Stephen was glad he couldn't understand it.

He returned to his alcove and ate hungrily. For a few minutes he felt better, then he felt a powerful urge to go to the toilet. There were some filthy latrines behind the ghats, but there were also relatively clean toilets in the tourist hotels.

He hesitated for a moment, then he chose the latrines. He no longer belonged in the white man's world.

Then, as he came out of the latrines, he saw Will. He was just a figure in the distance, but Stephen knew it was him, and he ran after him down the narrow alley, past cows munching at piles of rubbish, twisting and turning, then coming out into a bigger, crowded street. Will was still there, in front of him. Stephen could have easily caught up with him, but instead he slowed down. It wouldn't do for Will to think he had been trying to find him. The meeting had to look accidental. He walked sedately, getting his breath back, looking down and keeping an eye on Will with his peripheral vision.

Where was Stephanie? he wondered. Usually they went everywhere together.

Further up the street there were some cheap hotels. Will went into one of them and Stephen followed. Will went up some stairs, presumably to his room, so Stephen sat down in the ground floor restaurant. When Will came down, or Stephanie came in, it would look like an accidental meeting.

It was fortunate, in a way. He was not feeling so good today, and he needed time to settle his energies. Also he was still hungry.

The waiter came over – just a boy – and looked him up and down doubtfully.

Stephen hesitated. Since he gave his money away, he had only eaten what he had been given, but Will and Stephanie would pay, he was certain. He ordered a banana pancake and tea.

The pancake was thick and doughy with slices of hot banana sizzling on the top. He ate half of it and then felt sick.

He pushed it away. He was growing too pure for food.

Soon he would be able to live on air – but the pure air of the mountains, not the stench of this dirty city.

He would smoke no more chillums, he determined. They were a means to an end only, and he was nearing that end.

He shut his eyes and breathed into his nausea, and it eased. At the same time he felt the Kundalini rising again from the base of his spine, blissful and strong, dispelling all his doubts, his unease.

He remembered Stephanie's body and the way she had held him after they made love. Yet it had meant nothing to him. He was beyond attachment. He should teach that to Will too. Perhaps Will had not yet properly understood.

And Will was beautiful, more beautiful than Stephanie, with his soft lips and gentle ways. It was Will who attracted him in the first place. He felt a strong urge to see him.

Without thinking he left his bag by his seat, walked past the cash desk and up the stairs. He didn't know which room, so he knocked on doors. At the third one he heard Will's voice:

'What is it?'

'It's me,' said Stephen.

Will opened the door and let him in.

'Oh,' said Will when he saw Stephen, but he held the door open and Stephen walked in and sat on the single bed.

'Hi!' he said.

'How did you find me?' asked Will. He looked confused.

Stephen stared at him, letting his pupils dilate, so that Will couldn't help but meet his eyes.

'I knew where you'd be,' said Stephen softly.

But Will shook his head and pulled his eyes away.

'I'm sorry, Stephen, I think you should go...' he started to say.

'Where's Stephanie?'

'She...we decided to split up for a while, give ourselves some space. Just while we sort ourselves out. She's staying in the tourist bungalow.'

He stopped abruptly as if he'd already said more than he meant to.

'That's good!' said Stephen. 'You need to be on your own to grow sometimes.'

Will was still standing at the door, holding on to it as if about to make a sudden exit.

Stephen straightened his back, and smiled at him. Despite himself, Will smiled nervously back.

'God, you look rough, Stephen. Are you okay?'

'I'm fine. In fact I'm better than I've ever been.'

And he was. The presence of Will was like a tonic to him, and the boy's nervousness made him feel calm.

'I'm sorry, Stephen,' said Will. 'I...I don't really want to see you. I was just...writing a letter. Would you mind going?'

Stephen stood up.

'Sure,' he said. 'I'll wait for you in the restaurant.'

'No,' said Will, looking up at him with a great effort.

'No, I don't mean that . . . I mean, I don't want to see you again. Not at all. Not ever again. I know what you did. I found out. You got me stoned and then you slept with Stephanie. It's not right, and it hurt. That's why I've split up with her, don't you see, and I don't want to see you again either.'

There were tears in his eyes as he looked at Stephen almost pleading.

This time, Stephen held his eyes. He could still do it. He felt Will coming into him. He felt his own power growing.

It didn't matter what Will said, Will loved him really. He knew that for a certainty. Because Will could see him as he really was, see the God in him. They would forget about Stephanie. He and Will together, they would be powerful.

He stepped towards him.

'I did it for you,' he murmured. 'Believe me.'

'No!' said Will. 'NO!'

But he didn't look away. And gazing into Will's eyes, Stephen realised what he had known all along.

'Do you know who I am?' he asked. His eyes were focused on Will's, holding him tightly. 'I am Jesus. I am Buddha. I am Shiva. I will save you, Will.'

'Christ!' said Will. 'You're mad.'

'Believe me,' said Stephen. 'Believe in me,' and he gripped Will's shoulders and bent forward to kiss that soft beautiful mouth, for a moment allowing his eyes to close.

'Get out! Get out!' shouted Will, tearing himself away and pulling the door open.

Then something happened. Stephen looked at Will, and for a moment he was not in his body at all. He was not even in the room. He was not himself. He was nobody, but the body and mind he was in were Mr Wortle's and the person he was looking at was himself, Stephen, and what he was seeing was not just a beautiful boy, but his hope of salvation . . .

Time froze.

'*I is someone else*,' murmured Mr Wortle.

Then it was all over and there was nothing but emptiness, a terrifying abyss aching with longing.

Stephen felt he was going to suffocate. His breath came in pants, and his whole body was shaking. He tore off his clothes and threw them on the floor, and stood naked and pure. Nothing. He would have nothing. He would be pure as the Naga Babas, pure as the wind.

What had he done?

He didn't care any more. He was beyond caring.

Insects were buzzing around his head – he shook his hair, but they wouldn't go away.

He ran naked from the room and down the stairs.

He stopped in the street. Why was everyone staring at him? And where should he go? There was nowhere to go, and he was nothing. Nothing but movement and pain, and insects buzzing at his skull.

So he ran. He ran. The crowd made way for him and he ran.

As he ran he saw faces. He saw Rob. He saw Reuben. He saw Mary, and Ian. He saw Astrid. He saw Thomas the medical student, and Carl the junkie and Janey the girl in Istanbul.

What were they all doing here? But he hadn't time for that.

And then he saw his mother and his father. They were running beside him trying to talk to him, but he couldn't hear what they said, and he didn't want to, and he hadn't enough breath to tell his mother she had maggots in her mouth. His father was calling to him, and Stephen felt sorry for him, and the way the wind caught up his white hair revealing his bald patch. But he couldn't stop for him now.

Soon his parents were out of breath, and they fell back, and Stephen was running on his own through empty streets, then out onto a bridge that stretched forever.

It wasn't forever though: Mother Ganga rolled below him and beside him a freight train rattled across iron girders.

In the middle of the bridge he stopped. The crowd was still following, led by his parents, moving carefully because the bridge was unsteady and the footpath was narrow. But ahead of him, coming towards him from the other side, was another group: Grindlesham. He could see Soames, and Mr Husting his housemaster, and in front of them Mr Wortle in a cravat, smiling and holding out a copy of 'The Ballad of Reading Gaol'.

So they had come for him, even here. Deep down, he had always known they would.

The insects had caught up with him too, and were buzzing about his head.

The only way was up.

He climbed the girders beside him, till he reached a ledge where he could sit perched above the walkway. With a moment of sudden clarity he saw he was on the railway bridge that crossed the Ganges at the northern end of Benares. The train was still lumbering noisily over the tracks, and far below him the immense river flowed, brown and eternal.

He felt a drop and looked up. The sky was black above him, heavy with rain. Any minute and the clouds would burst. There were no birds. The people had disappeared too, or he was no longer conscious of them. Behind the rumble of the train there was an enormous stillness and silence.

He gazed back down at the river.

There was turbulence here in the middle, swirls and eddies, and objects carried down on the current: bits of wood, old cardboard boxes. Perhaps the torn up photo of his parents was floating through there at this moment. Perhaps there would be a dead body – he had heard there often were.

He watched intently.

And then something extraordinary happened. The surface broke, and out leapt two river dolphins, one behind the other, spinning in the air and then disappearing as though they had never been.

It was a signal. They were calling him.

He knew he had to join them.

It was easy. He would dive, head first, just like in the school swimming pool. He would fall through the air. He would meet the water. And then he would know forever the ultimate peace, the peace of God that passes all men's understanding.

He stood up and took a deep breath, stretching his arms out and then up, ready to dive. Behind him there was a tremendous flash of sheet lightning, and then a sudden gust of wind and the heavens opened and the rain poured down over everything, driving away the flies, cooling, flattening, cleansing.

Stephen held his position, balancing on that moment of time.

'Stephen! Hey, Stephen!'

He knew the voice, and looked back. The walkway below him was crowded with Indian faces, water dripping from their hair as they stared up at him. There was no sign of his parents or the Grindlesham mob, just Jerry, in a limp, wet, white cotton suit, calling up to him.

'Hey, Stephen, man, good to see you!'

It was good to see Jerry too. Good old Jerry. Someone he could trust in all this confusion.

'Hey, come on down, man, and I'll buy you a meal.'

'I'm going swimming with the dolphins,' said Stephen.

'Great idea, man, and I'll come with you, but, hey, we've got all day. Let's get a meal first. Come on, I'll help you down.'

Stephen lowered his arms and started to move, but then he stopped himself. The Indian faces were friendly and not threatening. Jerry too. But he had seen what he had seen.

'My parents,' he said. 'The school... They're coming for me.'

'No worries, man,' said Jerry. 'I'll look after you. Hell, I was the one who got you here, wasn't I? Anyway, your parents love you, you know that.'

'The school...' said Stephen. 'Mr Wortle, Soames, the rest of them. They're here. I saw them a minute ago.'

'Well they're not here now. Hey, Stevie, come on down, man. I'm starving.'

Stephen looked down at the river, its surface pock-marked by the rain. He looked up at the black clouds, and along the shoreline of Benares to the burning ghats, where a plume of smoke survived the downpour. Then he looked the other way, across the river to the open country beyond, the green fields and mud huts of little settlements.

He wanted it all.

But there was something he wanted more than that now, more than anything, and Jerry knew.

'It's okay, man,' said Jerry softly, stretching out his hand to help him down. 'I'll look after you. I'll take you home.'

Chapter 22

Nothing much had changed.

After the first emotional greetings, his mother's tears, his father's formal handshake, after the visits to the doctor, and the barber, and the shoe shop, everything settled back to old routines. Jerry left him at the airport, fading into the shadows as his mother rushed in to claim him, and then there was nobody to talk to about Afghanistan, or the Green Bus, or the Blue Mosque... It was as if it had all never been.

Except that Rob sent postcards, occasionally.

It was autumn. His mother spent her days pruning roses and going to meetings of the Conservative Party. She had just been selected to stand for the County Council, and was enjoying her new role. His father went to work and came home and said little, politely.

Stephen ate well, and began to put on weight again. His mother had been shocked at first by how thin he was, but to him everybody in England seemed fat. Nonetheless he enjoyed her food and enjoyed the pleasure she took in feeding him. Only once, when she made a Victoria sponge cake with cream and jam, did he refuse, unable to explain his sudden overpowering aversion.

He stayed a lot in his room, studying. The autumn term had started, but there was no thought of sending him back to Grindlesham. They probably wouldn't have had him anyway. Instead he enrolled at the local technical college. He liked it, and he was starting to make friends. There were girls there too; one of them with ash blonde hair and long fingers, who reminded him – just a little bit – of Astrid.

At first his mother was tense with him, as if at any moment he might disappear all over again, but after a few weeks she relaxed. His father was gentler, though distant. One evening he said to Stephen:

'Your mother's much better, now that we hear from Rob sometimes. I suppose we've got you to thank for that, haven't we?'

But that was as far as he went. He never asked Stephen about his travels. Perhaps he saw them as a disreputable episode to be ashamed of, or perhaps, since he had never talked about his experiences abroad, he didn't expect Stephen to either. It was probably just as well.

At first, Stephen wanted to ask his mother why she had lied to him about Rob's letter, but when it came to it, he couldn't. He had to accept her, and he had to accept the gulf between them. It was just how she was.

No one would have called it a happy household, but at least it was a peaceful one, and that was what he needed: a place to rest, to assimilate, to recover in mind and body.

Stephen's memory of his last weeks in India was hazy. He knew now that he had had some sort of breakdown, and his consciousness had become fragmented, like a dream: dislocated images, reality and hallucination jumbled together. But Jerry had brought him home. Jerry, who had got him into the situation in the first place, had got him out of it too. He had taken Stephen to Delhi, sorted out new papers from the Embassy, bought him a ticket, sat next him on the plane, and then disappeared – off to see Astrid again, in Germany, or so he'd said.

He had a kilo of hash with him, sewn into his waist-coat, to pay for it all.

Rob had been with him some of the time in India, too. He must have helped to get him back. Stephen could remember his face, sometimes comforting, sometimes frightening, but always dreamlike.

Then on the aeroplane a stewardess with a plastic smile handed him a plastic tray of plastic food, and he blinked and something shifted in his brain. The dream had ended. He was awake. He turned to Jerry, who saw the different expression in his eyes and grinned.

'What a long hard trip it's been, huh?'

Now he sat in a pub in a small town, sipping a lemonade. His once pudgy face was thin, and there was an assurance in his eyes that made him seem older than his sixteen years. It was lunch time and the pub was nearly empty. He had chosen a quiet corner and waited patiently.

The pub smelled of beer and tobacco, as pubs do. A log effect fire flickered in an imitation inglenook. It had been chosen by Mr Wortle. Stephen had written to him, asking to meet him, and he had written back, suggesting a time and place.

Stephen had come by train and walked to the pub, arriving early. He was glad he was there first – he wanted time to prepare himself. He sat quietly, getting used to the place, looking and listening, and sipping his drink. A man at the bar was telling a rambling story to a bored barmaid. She glanced at Stephen occasionally as if she would rather be talking to him, but he avoided any eye contact.

The door opened. Stephen felt a flicker of anticipation. It was him. It was Mr Wortle.

He was wearing a tweed jacket and a cravat. He saw Stephen immediately and came over.

'My dear boy, how *are* you?'

He held out his hand. Stephen didn't take it. He couldn't bring himself to touch Mr Wortle at all.

Mr Wortle dropped it again rather sheepishly.

'Let me buy you a drink.'

'I've already got one,' said Stephen.

'Then you won't mind if I buy myself one.'

Mr Wortle went over to the bar. Stephen watched his back as he talked to the barmaid. He could see from his movements that Mr Wortle was nervous – more nervous than he was. After all, the Wart didn't know why he had asked to meet him – not that he really knew that himself.

Mr Wortle sat down with his gin and tonic, and smiled warmly, crinkling up his eyes in the same way he had always done.

'So, what have you been up to? I'm told you've been half way round the world. Afghanistan. India. How absolutely marvellous. Tell me all about it. I'm longing to hear.'

With a shock, Stephen realised that Mr Wortle was the first person who had asked him about his journey since he got back. Was it a bluff, or did he really want to know? Did he really think that that was what Stephen had come to talk about?

Stephen had learned from the Sadhus the power of silence. He watched Mr Wortle and said nothing.

'Did you meet your brother in far-off lands? If so, I hope you gave him my regards.'

For a moment, Stephen was tempted to carry on as Mr Wortle seemed to want, as if nothing had happened between them, to go back to the beginning, before that visit to Stratford. Then he could tell him the whole story, and Mr Wortle would listen, all sweet attention, in the way his mother never could.

He couldn't hate him. Not now that he was in front of him. He felt sorry for him really, this funny old queer with greying temples and a cravat.

But he couldn't forget what he had done either. Never. Not in his whole life.

'Yes,' he said. 'I did meet Rob. And I told him about you. Everything.'

There was a silence.

Mr Wortle examined his drink.

'I see,' he said at last. 'And what did he say?'

'It doesn't matter what he said,' said Stephen, with sudden intensity. 'He won't report you, if that's what you mean. He's in India anyway, and he's not coming back. It's what *I* say that matters. And who I say it to.'

Mr Wortle met his gaze. His face was white, but his eyes were direct.

'That's not what I meant, Stephen. I'm not afraid of what anyone says – well, I am, yes, I'm terrified, but I'll face it and I won't lie or deny. I know I . . . did wrong. Probably. But I was sincere. Believe me, I was always sincere.'

'What?' Stephen felt a rush of blood to the face. 'When you buggered me in the hotel bedroom, you were *sincere*?'

'Always,' said Mr Wortle. 'I don't think you ever understood, Stephen. You see, I loved you. I still do. You probably think I'm just a pervy schoolmaster who seduces boys all the time, but it's not like that. Not like that at all. I like boys, I admit it. I enjoy their company, I like to teach them, but with you it was something else—'

'I don't believe you,' interrupted Stephen. 'You had it all planned, didn't you – the trip to Stratford in the snow. You knew the weather forecast. I bet you'd even booked the hotel room in advance.'

Mr Wortle's lip was twitching, but he didn't deny it.

'I trusted you,' Stephen continued. 'You were like another father to me. A fine father figure, gratifying yourself on a gullible fifteen-year-old – why did you have to do it? Why did you have to spoil it all? If you really loved me you'd never have touched me.'

'Love and touch, they go together,' murmured Mr Wortle. 'That was all I wanted at first, to touch you, to hold you, but passion has a terrible power. I'm sorry, Stephen . . .'

'*Sorry*?' Stephen snorted.

Mr Wortle's body was slumped and his face was trembling. He was close to breaking down, but he pulled himself together and managed a tight, ironic smile.

'I am sorry. It's not enough I know. But I *am* sorry. I hurt you, I can see that, when all I wanted was your love. You're going to tell the police, aren't you? And I shall go to prison. I don't mind. It's only what I deserve. I shall miss the Aesthetes, though. It's true, isn't it, that each man kills the thing he loves?'

'No,' said Stephen. 'It's a lie. That isn't love. You don't know what love is.'

He stood up and left. In the street, he paused. The image of Mr Wortle's face came back to him with that tight smile. Stephen closed his eyes and the image became solider, the smiler broader, more insidious. He breathed deeply a few times and felt his energy gather at the base of his spine as he gathered his focus. Then he watched as the face dissolved, like the Cheshire Cat, slowly, the smile last.

It was his father he told in the end. His mother was often out now in the evenings, at political meetings – the elections were imminent. One evening when he and his father were alone in the house, Stephen went down to his study. His father was working on some papers, but he took his glasses off and smiled at Stephen when he came in.

'How's the homework?'

'I've done it,' said Stephen.

Neither of them could think of anything else to say, so his father put his glasses back on and returned to his paperwork. There was a nice atmosphere in the study. Everything was solid and well used. Stephen sat in the old armchair and watched his father working, as he had done as a child, so many years ago.

'Are you all right?' his father asked after a while. 'Do you want anything? Get yourself a drink if you like. Some beer?'

'No thanks,' said Stephen. 'Dad... Could I talk to you about something? Something about Grindlesham?'

'Yes of course,' said his father. 'What is it? Fire away!'

He took out his pipe and started to fill it.

Stephen told it all – or nearly all – and his father listened, touching his lip with his pipe stem but never smoking it, hardly moving behind his desk.

When Stephen had finished, he said quietly:

'Yes. Thank you for telling me. I don't think we should tell your mother though, for the moment, do you? It would upset her too much.'

He came out from behind his desk and leant against the front of it, thinking.

'It's appalling. A man like that. Who'd have thought it? I'll have to do something, of course. Stephen, do you think Mr Wortle... does he do it all the time, or was it just...?'

Stephen shook his head.

'I don't know. I think it was just me. I feel sorry for him really. I mean, I can see how it happened. Anyone could be like that, in a way. But I don't want him to go to prison, Dad. That wouldn't help anybody.'

'All right,' said his father. 'Then I'll talk to the school. They'll deal with it quietly.'

There was a silence. An awkward silence that hung between them, neither looking at the other. Stephen was about to get up and say, 'Well, I'd better get on with my homework then,' when his father reached out and put his hand clumsily on Stephen's head.

'It wasn't your fault,' he said quietly. 'Don't ever think it was your fault.'

Stephen turned towards him.

'You know I love you,' said his father awkwardly. 'Your mother and I, we both love you. And Rob. Whatever happens and always.'

And then Stephen was in his arms, and holding him tight.

Crying and crying and crying.

Sweet tears, like a baby's.

Acknowledgements

I dug around everywhere to find the material for this story - not least in my own memories and those of my friends — and all the works of fact and fiction that influenced me would make a long list. But two books in particular provided essential reference points: Graham Robb's excellent biography, *Rimbaud* (Picador), and David Tomory's wonderful compilation of travellers' tales from the 60s and 70s, *A Season in Heaven* (Lonely Planet).

To these, and all the many others who helped me write this book, many thanks.

The author and publishers gratefully acknowledge permission to reprint extracts from the following books and poems as follows:

'Howl' from *Allen Ginsberg: Collected Poems 1947–1980* (Viking, 1985. First published in *Howl and Other Poems*, 1956). Copyright © Allen Ginsberg 1956, 1984.

Hermann Hesse *Journey to the East* (Peter Owen Publishers Ltd., London, 1956).

Eric Newby *A Short Walk in the Hindu Kush* (HarperCollins Publishers Ltd.). Copyright © Eric Newby 1958.

Dylan Thomas 'Fern Hill' from *Collected Poems* (J. M. Dent, 1946).

W. B. Yeats 'Byzantium' and 'Sailing to Byzantium' (A. P. Watt Ltd. on behalf of Michael B. Yeats)

Lyrics from 'When the music's over' (Morrison/ Densmore/Kriegar/Manzarek) © 1967 by kind permission of Universal Music Publishing Ltd.